The Man Who Killed
Caravaggio

by
Jerome D. Oremland, M.D.

Order this book online at www.trafford.com
or email orders@trafford.com

Most Trafford titles are also available at major online book retailers.

Printed in the United States of America.

ISBN: 978-1-4269-6088-8 (sc)
ISBN: 978-1-4269-6089-5 (hc)
ISBN: 978-1-4269-6090-1 (e)

Library of Congress Control Number: 2011903751

Trafford rev. 07/25/2011

 www.trafford.com

North America & international
toll-free: 1 888 232 4444 (USA & Canada)
phone: 250 383 6864 ♦ fax: 812 355 4082

Table of Contents

Acknowledgements

This book arose out of numerous wonderful visits to museums and churches in London, Rome, Florence, Naples, Sicily, and Malta. Everywhere I met sextons, curators, and art historians who patiently guided me on my quest to learn more about the life and death of Caravaggio.

Of great service in this endeavor has been my friendship with my colleague Domenico Neschi, M.D., who through the years has invited me as a professor to lecture to his students at the International Institute for Psychoanalytic Research in Rome. These annual visits to Italy have provided me with great joy for over twenty years and more than a casual acquaintanceship with the city of Rome.

Guia Bargigli, a guide in Rome, has been a helpful companion on some of my adventures in and around Rome. With uncanny ability, she gains access to rooms that are closed and makes sure I do not meet too many *chiuso per restauro* signs.

My colleague in Pavia, Alberto Cevini, Ph.D., helped me in making museum contacts and translating my requests. Patiently, he drove me around and around until we finally located the village of Caravaggio. He and I were both surprised and delighted that the man we asked for directions turned out to be the husband of the last surviving member of the Caravaggio family.

In Malta I had the good fortune to meet a young priest, whose name I did not record, who quickened by my interest in Caravaggio and Michelangelo invited me deeply into the bowels of the Saint Paul Cathedral in Mdina. There he showed me and translated, sometimes shyly blushing, original transcriptions of a Caravaggio interview with the Inquisition.

As with my previous manuscripts, my son Noah, always eager to show me distracting hyperbole and sentimentality, sharpened my writing. My daughter Celia Teter, the invaluable editor, read numerous versions of the manuscript with a keen eye toward increasing clarity, avoiding redundancy, and correcting grammatical error.

Christine Walsh-Newton laboriously set the manuscript and the illustrations to fit the demands of modern printing. My young Italian artist friend, Milos Maiorana-Zahrodka, helped add color to the language of the book.

Wendy Zieger of Bridgeman Art Library, New York, kindly arranged for permission to use illustrations from that library's excellent archives. Although there is considerable controversy about many of the dates and titles of the paintings, I have followed

ACKNOWLEDGEMENTS

the Bridgeman system. Art Resources, New York, provided the image and permission for *Saint Francis in Ecstasy.*

I am particularly grateful to Lisa Steindler, actor and director, for her encouraging and insightful comments.

Even though Caravaggio painted scarcely nineteen years, so vast are his complete works that it is only possible here to provide representations of a few great pieces. To aid in the visualization, each chapter opens with a painting that epitomizes a period in Caravaggio's life. It is my sincere hope that readers will correlate my writing with the excellent Caravaggio website, www.caravaggio.com, and the many beautifully illustrated books that brilliantly show the color and interacting forms that comprise the complete Caravaggio catalog.

—JDO

Caravaggio, *The Young Bacchus*, 1597

Chapter One

Caravaggio

J can hardly believe that I knew Caravaggio. We met in 1593, really as boys. I was scarcely 16 and he, 21, although he lied and said he was 19. In those days, the younger you were the better if you wanted to be a painter. To think he was to become the most sought after and revered painter of his time in all of Italy. Yet when I first met him, I knew that he was headed for tragedy.

I am Mario Minniti, and I write this in 1640 when I am approaching 63. Everyone knew that Caravaggio's death was mysterious. Some say that he died of fever; others say that he was murdered. I know what happened. For fear of my life for thirty years I have had to hold my tongue. Now when many are dead, I want to tell the story—the story that I know to be true. I do not know who will read this, but I want a record to exist.

First, I will tell you a bit about me. I am Sicilian, born on 8 December 1577. I am a painter, and over the last thirty years I have developed an excellent reputation in Italy, especially in Sicily. You may even know my most important work; actually it is my best work, *The Miracle at Naim,* in Messina.

Caravaggio taught me a lot, but I think I developed a distinctive style. There is no question though that I benefited enormously from my association with him. With passing years his name has become increasingly magical not only in Italy but all over Europe. I know that collectors like to have works by those few of us who were directly associated with him.

At times I am labeled a *caravaggista,* a student or disciple of Caravaggio. I am proud of that, yet anyone who knew Caravaggio will tell you that he was so individualistic and difficult to get along with that it was impossible to be his student let alone his disciple. What is best to say is that all *caravaggisti* are followers.

I have my detractors. Some unkind critics have even called me a copyist and a parasite. What hurt most are those who refer to my paintings as "endlessly recycled motifs." I don't know what they expect from someone who paints largely religious *istoria,* which in Italy are the largest part of the commissions that I and most artists receive today.

I do not claim to be a great painter, but I have an excellent workshop with able assistants. I think I have mastered the style *di maniera,* the Mannerist style, with its idealizing of life and spiritualizing of being, and blended and moderated it with the realism that Caravaggio initiated. Yet my blend, and Caravaggio would be very critical of it for this, is designed not to ruffle the feathers of those responsible for religious commissions because in Italy today, and especially in Sicily, there is much concern with the restrictions on religious thought imposed by the Council of Trent over seventy years ago. These restrictions greatly affect art. It is enough to say that there are rules about what you can and cannot paint. For example, they explicitly state that "all lasciviousness be avoided … that figures shall not be painted with a beauty exciting to lust … nothing (can be) profane or indecorous … pagan imagery must be avoided." I must say that they do like the saints' eyes rolled up in ecstasy (or I add facetiously in *organismo*), and you can only get away with showing any flesh if it is an act of torture.

I learned early on that being radical in your representation of the sacred ones is asking for trouble and cancelled commissions, a problem that plagued Caravaggio throughout his lifetime. Even though these "rules" were made long ago and are now somewhat more relaxed except in Sicily, they are a continuing problem. Although far from Rome, culturally and religiously Sicily is a very conservative country.

Besides being conservative, Sicily, once a proud and very wealthy independent kingdom, now is and I think always will be poor. Since the twelfth century, the time of its greatness, Sicily has been endlessly ravaged by wars, invaders, and corruption, and there is always the problem of the heat and drought. It is not easy to live in Sicily or to be successful here, and yet art, especially religious art, continues to thrive.

My father died when I was 15, and I decided to leave Sicily to go to Rome. My collectors like to say that I went to Rome to study art. That is quite a stretch of the facts. Actually, I was always in trouble as a child and young man. Unfortunately, I liked confrontations and fights. I was constantly fighting with my father about the most trivial matters, and I was known as a trouble maker and "wild." After my father's death, my mother was more than glad that I "ran away" to Rome.

I am not proud of it, but I never saw my family again after I left Sicily. Even when I returned twenty years later, I never sought out any of them. To this day, I do not know how they fared.

I do have good memories of the nuns who vainly tried to educate and "tame" me. Although not at the time, I am now thankful that they instilled in me good, grammatically correct Italian that I am currently using as I write this. Actually during my childhood and teens, mostly I spoke Sicilian dialect. After I "moved" to Rome, I was pretty good in Roman dialect. In truth, it was the raw language of the Roman streets (that I will spare you, my unknown reader) that was my language until I returned to Sicily and became an "established refined" older painter. Over the years, I have matured a lot. I learned how to compromise and please so as to be successful. Compromise was a word completely unknown to Caravaggio.

My getting to Rome was fateful in my meeting Caravaggio. I considered crossing the narrow straits of Messina into Reggio di Calabria and working my way up to Rome. It would not have been too difficult for a young boy to get a ride on passing carts, but it would entail a lot of walking and finding jobs on the way.

Fate was to have it differently. At the port in Messina, I ran into a ship's captain. He must have been about 50 years old. He offered to take me to Rome if I would help him on the ship as a hand. It seemed like a gift from heaven.

It was a small cargo boat, and I was to help with the sails and loading and unloading the cargo. It was not until the first night aboard that I learned what the cost of my passage was really to be. The captain approached me in a way that was clear what he wanted. I felt I had no choice and submitted. At first it hurt and I felt degraded, but I must confess that before long I realized that I had a profession. It was this newly acquired profession that was to carry me into some extraordinary situations, including meeting Caravaggio.

I don't want to sound apologetic, but I must say that that "work" never seemed natural to me. It was always a job and an unpleasant one; yet, one that I had to do. I quickly add that eventually I married and had a family. In fact I married twice, but that is another story and one that involved Caravaggio in Malta.

It was close to ten miserable days before our small boat put in at the port near Civitavecchia. On the way, we stopped a short time in Naples. What a beautiful city it was. I could tell it was bustling with commerce and excitement. I considered abandoning the boat and staying on, but the *vecchiaccio* kept the boat tied to an offshore buoy and would not let me off. Reports that Rome was alive with re-building encouraged me to continue my ordeal with my "teacher." I must say it was a great relief when we finally reached Civitavecchia and I said good-bye to my "teacher" skipper. I do not think he ever learned my name. I was always *il ragazzino,* "the kid."

Civitavecchia was a beehive of activity. Everywhere there were ships unloading material and bringing laborers. The talk was of nothing but the rebuilding of the churches and palaces of Rome. I felt a renewed confidence that I had made a good choice in going to Rome. Surely, I would find work there. In the back of my mind, rather vaguely, was the idea that I might be able to pursue my art talent, which the good nuns told me I had and was wasting.

Rome had suffered terribly in 1527 from Emperor Charles V's occupation and was slowly recovering. By the time I arrived, the city echoed with the sounds of hammers and saws. The restoring and building were intoxicating.

I had little or no interest in politics or religion. Gregory, Sixtus, Urban, Innocent, and Clement were only names to me, but I was smart enough to see that the Vatican and the clerical hierarchy were the source of power, wealth, and most importantly, work. Even from my view from the streets, I could feel the intense desire to re-populate Rome with magnificent palaces, public buildings, and churches. The Vatican was determined to return Rome to its original glory and place as the head of the Catholic Church.

Religious ambassadors from many Catholic countries came to Rome and vied to outdo each other and the Roman hierarchy itself in the raising of sumptuous palaces and residences. Everywhere construction workers, architects, and painters, especially those who could do frescoes, were needed to design, construct, and decorate the massive palaces and churches.

On the wharves in Civitavecchia all the young fellows

talked about the *rione* of the Campo Marzio with its playing field, the brothels around the Mausoleum of Augustus, and especially the lively Piazza Navona. Immediately, I headed there.

Indeed, the *rione* was an exciting place. Quickly I could see that the scene was overwhelmingly young men. The streets and *piazze* were filled with mercenaries, discharged soldiers, servants, and vagabonds. Everyone seemed to be from somewhere else. Although outlawed, knives, swords, and daggers were everywhere, and there was constant fighting over nothing. Any fight was sure to gather a large and cheering crowd. As I mentioned I was rather wild, as my father and the nuns labeled me. Coming from Sicily and being "wild," I knew a good deal about life on the streets. Yet, I must say that Sicily was tame compared to Rome. I loved it.

The playing field was a large area formerly used for military drills and now entirely devoted to various sports activities. Here men vigorously and furiously arm wrestled, body wrestled, and ran various kinds of races. The main sport was tennis in which a pliable ball was hit with an open hand back and forth between the contestants. Everything carried a wager. You could be sure that each contest ended not in acclaimed victory but in arguments, fights, and sometimes riots.

In the *rione* were many taverns with wonderful names like

the Taverna del Lupo, the Taverna del Toro, and the Taverna del Blackamoor. Numerous brothels clustered around the Mausoleum of Augustus. The elegant ones were frequented by noblemen, "celibate" Church hierarchy, ambassadors, and well-to-do businessmen, mostly bankers. Around the Mausoleum occasionally one could see the grand courtesans, really beautiful girls. I was astonished to learn that most were 16 or younger.

During the day, the Piazza Navona was filled with acrobats, jugglers, bear fighting, and many street artists painting, drawing, and selling their art. Floating everywhere were street whores, boys and girls, looking for tricks to take into the alleys off the Piazza. Prostitution must have been the second largest business in Rome, second only to the Church.

At night, gangs of hoodlums carrying torches paraded through the streets on their way to the Piazza raucously singing in unison and looking for trouble. If the daylight hours seemed crowded with hookers and hustlers, the nighttime Piazza literally crawled with them.

From day one in Rome, I knew that my new-found profession was the one that was going to sustain me. There was no shortage of men, especially older men, looking for a *puttano*. With my sweet, young, cherubic face, I found it all too easy to find a dark corner or a bed and an unwanted but paying companion on any given night.

I staked out a territory near the Fontana del Moro in the south end of the Piazza. Being a Sicilian, I liked the idea of being near the Moor and dark-skinned people.

I am not sure how long I had been in Rome lackadaisically looking for work and largely hustling when I noted sitting at the fountain's edge a short, dark, heavy eye-lidded young man with thick dark eyebrows and unruly black hair. He looked ill. I thought he was Sicilian and spoke to him in Sicilian dialect, but I quickly learned that he was from northern Italy. That chance meeting was to become an unbelievably fateful event.

We met occasionally in the Piazza. He told me that he was an artist and that he made a small living painting still lifes and simple street scenes to sell in the Piazza. He said that he was 19 and had come to Rome because there was much artist work available in Rome. I lied and said that was why I was there too. We both knew that each was lying and that we actually made our livings on the hustle. If I were a reluctant hustler, he was a morose one. But, we both knew that that is what we had to do.

We ran into each other a number of times. I liked to watch him paint and noted that he didn't draw but painted directly on his small canvases. Easily I could see that he had unusual talent. His still lifes of fruits and vegetables had a luscious, almost erotic life in them. I liked to draw and took to drawing near him and sold some work. That encouraged me enormously.

In the beginning, he was difficult to talk with. I learned that his name was Michelangelo Merisi, but in Rome he was called Caravaggio because he came from the small village of Caravaggio not far from Milan. Always he was surly, unkempt, and unclean, but I was drawn to him. Even though occasionally our relationship was sexual, in looking back, I think the true bond was that we were both lost souls hanging onto each other. It is how we survived.

Sometimes we would talk into the early hours of the morning. It wasn't long before he confessed that in fact he was 21. He said that he had learned to lie about his age — "old men really like their artists and their *puttani* young."

I was surprised to learn that he had recently left the studio of the famous and infamous artist Guiseppe Cesari. He joked that if the life of the hustler were "hell," it was "heaven" compared with working for Cesari. Caravaggio's anger would mount as he described how Cesari abused assistants. He added that he paid "next to nothing" and even worse, the bread he served was stale and the meat and vegetables usually rotten.

THE MAN WHO KILLED CARAVAGGIO

Caravaggio said that when Cesari was elevated to *cavaliere* by His Holiness Clement VIII, "If he were bad before, he became insufferably contemptuous after." In a mocking tone, he imitated Cesari, "I am now to be known as Cavaliere d'Arpino, Arpino being the place of my father's birth." *Cavaliere*, an ancient title, literally means horse rider, but we knew that he was from a different part of the horse.

We thought Cesari a mediocre talent who knew how to please using a moderated Mannerist style. He was a genius at not offending and was always careful not to cross the increasingly imposed Council of Trent restrictions on art. Although only 25, he had insinuated himself into the good grace of not only His Holiness Sextus V, but even more so with Clement VIII.

In truth, we all were both contemptuous and envious of Cesari. I must admit that he was a handsome man with aristocratic good looks. He had a fine aquiline nose, and his carefully groomed moustache and small pointed beard made us look like the coarse and scummy street rats we were. It must be added that Cesari was a man of great and productive energy.

Actually, Caravaggio perfected his still-life skills doing still lifes for D'Arpino. He was irked that he had to leave several paintings with D'Arpino. He said it was really extortion to get out of the apprentice contract. Among the paintings that he left was a strange painting that Caravaggio himself disliked, a self-portrait he did shortly after he left the Ospedale Santa Maria della Consolazione. The painting is now called *Il Bacchino Malato*. I was never able to get a straight story from Caravaggio, but apparently he spent nearly a year in the Ospedale recovering from some unrelenting illness he contracted when he first came to Rome.

I believe D'Arpino kept a third painting. I mention these paintings because they are involved in a bitter and ironic fate. Knowing how D'Arpino lost ownership of these paintings and just how the Cardinal Borghese got them reassures me that there is justice, albeit a twisted one.

D'Arpino was to play a major role in some events that changed Caravaggio and my life in ways unimaginably for the better. Let me be clear though, in no way was that good fortune intended by him. He also played a major role in much of the unhappiness Caravaggio later was to endure.

Caravaggio and I did grow closer despite his quarrelsomeness and dour bitterness. Always he treated me as *il ragazzino* and the mignon; I must admit that in every way, including sexually, I was subservient to him. Yet over time a strong bond developed, and Caravaggio told me a good deal about his early life, although I am not sure of the facts. Caravaggio was rather flamboyant, self-excusing, and not addicted to the truth. But I will attempt to piece together as best I can what he told me with what I heard from fellow artists and friends of ours.

His father's name was Fermo Merisi, and he may have been a lower grade architect to the great Sforza family in Milan. It may be that Fermo also managed some of the Sforza property around Caravaggio, where his wife's family also owned property. Caravaggio said his father had some ability to draw, particularly to draft, well.

Caravaggio's mother, Lucia Aratori, was Fermo's second wife and from a well-regarded family. His first wife, Maddalena Vacchi, died in childbirth. There must have been close ties to the Sforza family because Caravaggio mentioned that the Marchese Francesco da Caravaggio, a Sforza, was a signed witness to his parents' marriage.

Whether that were true or not, I do not know. Caravaggio liked to elevate his family's importance. What I do know is that the Colonna family and particularly Marchesa Costanza Colonna, Francesco's child bride, became a constant patron and protector throughout Caravaggio's life. What is of importance is that the Marchesa and her family's influence extended far north into Genoa and south deeply beyond Naples and even into Malta.

I know Caravaggio had a brother, Giovan Battista, who I think was about two years younger than Caravaggio. I know that he was at the Jesuit Collegio Romano and became a Jesuit priest. Caravaggio once mentioned that his brother had sought him out shortly after Caravaggio came to Rome. I do not know what occasioned the visit, but Caravaggio told me that the visit "did not go well." I could not believe it when Caravaggio told me, "I greeted him with, 'I don't know you.'" I never learned what was the source of the antagonism, but I thought it must have had to do with what Caravaggio had done with the money they had inherited when their mother died. I had inkling that Caravaggio had squandered the money, or at least so it was thought by his brother and sister. I never heard Caravaggio speak of Giovan Battista again.

I know there was a younger sister, who I believe was named Caterina. Caravaggio mentioned that she married and moved from Caravaggio to Como with her husband. He mentioned that her children would be the only possible continuance of the Merisi family. I also believe there may have been a brother, possibly a stepbrother, who died as a child.

Caravaggio told me that he was born on the feast day of San Michele Archangelo and that is why he was named Michelangelo.

THE MAN WHO KILLED CARAVAGGIO

He liked to say, "Little did they know that I would be a painter greater than the Divine Michelangelo."

As I mentioned, Caravaggio was born in 1571, not 1573 as he told everyone and as was reported in his epitaph by an artist friend Giovanni Milesi. I think he was born in Milan. Sometimes he said he was born in the village of Caravaggio and that he and his family moved back to Milan after his birth. He did say that because of the threat of the plague in Milan, in 1577 the family quickly moved from Milan to his mother's family's small farm in Caravaggio. The move was not successful because both his grandfather Bernardino and his father died in Caravaggio of the plague when Caravaggio was 6. Caravaggio said that they died within hours of each other, but that may be part of his tendency to be dramatic. He often called himself an orphan, but that also may be part of his dramatic nature. What was true was that he felt himself alone in the world.

It is all a little unclear, but I know that when he was 13, Caravaggio was apprenticed to Simone Pederasini in Milan for four years. Poor Pederasini, he undoubtedly had a struggle on his hands most of the time. Although Caravaggio was always unruly, disrespectful, and given to argument even as a boy, the old master was able to teach Caravaggio much of the style of the great Titian and other great Lombardy painters. It probably was in the tradition of Titian that Caravaggio painted directly onto his canvases, never drawing, sketching, or pre-transferring his designs. The four-year apprenticeship with Pederasini was probably the only "commitment" that Caravaggio ever completed.

Like Titian, Caravaggio never signed his paintings. Arrogantly he quoted Titian, "They can tell it is mine from the way it is painted." The exception was a very late painting, *The Beheading of Saint John the Baptist,* painted in 1607 in Malta. It is signed in the spilled blood of the Baptist.

Throughout his life, Caravaggio disliked drawing and fresco, even though painting frescos was the most sought after medium to cover the walls of the great buildings. In fact, I can think of only one fresco Caravaggio ever did, the ceiling in a casino for His Eminence, Cardinal del Monte. It was oil-on-plaster, and I must say that his heart was not in it.

In his mid-teens, Caravaggio's mother died. Here the story gets really vague because I believe he was in prison in Milan for a year. At times the rumor in Rome was that he had killed a man in Milan; others said that he was imprisoned due to family indebtedness after his mother died. As close as we two became, Caravaggio never confided in me why he was in prison or the effect that that episode had had on him. Clearly though, I am sure the move to Rome was an attempt to get away from something.

Caravaggio came to Rome around 1592, penniless, alone, and already believing he was an artist of considerable ability. He was befriended by a Sicilian artist whom I never met called Lorenzo and later by Prospero Orsi, an artist with a peculiar specialty. Orsi was a master of Manneristic grotesques. This was a good connection for commissions for Caravaggio. Through the years, although often tried to the limit by Caravaggio, Orsi proved to be a faithful and reliable friend to both of us. It was probably through Orsi that Caravaggio came to be involved with Cesari.

In our early friendship, with the hardships we also shared an exciting life. It was a time of drinking, gambling, rowdy behavior, and many, many fights. We knew a lot of street people, retainers, servants, thieves, wanderers, artists, and models. Most of the girls were prostitutes, really beautiful and wonderful.

Sports played a big part in the way Caravaggio and all of us spent our time. The contests usually ended in brawls, fist fights, rock fights, and stabbings. Even though carrying arms was strictly illegal, I rarely saw Caravaggio (and many others) without a sword or dagger. He, unlike me, was an excellent swordsman, swift with the dagger, and a ferocious fighter. Often we were hauled away by the police, but the charges were usually dismissed.

CARAVAGGIO

We painted, actually Caravaggio painted and I mostly drew, in the Piazza Navona. The Piazza was a vital marketplace for art, and customers seemed to like to buy a painting that they had watched being created. I largely did sketches that were likenesses. I must admit I was pretty good at limning characteristics of my subjects, and Caravaggio said that he thought I had the makings of an artist.

The *rione* was a life made for Caravaggio and for me. Yet with the wisdom of advanced years, I hesitate to think what might have happened had it not been for an art dealer known as Costantino.

Costantino had a small shop across from the great Palazzo Madama on the Corso del Rinscimento just off the Corsia Agonale, an alley that led onto the Piazza Navona. Costantino liked the wild life of the *rione* and frequently visited the Piazza looking at the work of the street artists plying their trade. I am sure he was also looking for girls. As I mentioned Caravaggio and I liked to set up our easels at the end of the Piazza near the Fontana del Moro where Costantino spotted some of Caravaggio's work. After much discussion and I think some consultation with Orsi, Costantino approached Caravaggio with the idea of introducing him to the Cardinal del Monte. This introduction was to change art forever.

Caravaggio, *Saint Francis in Ecstasy*, 1595

Chapter Two

Cardinal del Monte

As it turned out, His Eminence, Cardinal Francesco Maria Borbone del Monte, a relative of the French royal family, a descendent of Julius III, and an eminent papal diplomat was a *frocio,* a fag. Forgive me for returning to the language of the street when I had promised to use my best literary form, but in doing the work that sustained me early in Rome I was always astonished at how many high-ranking clerics were my clients.

Rather boldly they would pick me up off the street and take me into their extraordinary palaces. Never did they ask my name. Sometimes we would just sit and talk for hours. They loved to hear about my life on the streets and my activities with my "clients." I obliged, making up some wonderful adventures and steamy exploits. Often they wanted to undress me or for me to undress them. It was astonishing how often they wanted to be spanked. Sometimes what they wanted was more involved, and they would ask me to inflict on them various kinds of pain. Some asked me to choke them. I was quite leery of these sadistic torments because I feared my client would die and I would be in serious trouble.

Many, including Del Monte, wanted to be held and rocked like a baby. One thing you learned quickly in this trade was how many sides there are to the rich and powerful.

We already knew something of Del Monte's sexual interest through widespread rumors from the prostitutes in the *rione*, where he was well-known. Most of the older women remembered that he often visited them in his younger days, but they noted a peculiarity. They said he always seemed more interested in talking with them about what they did with other men than in what he wanted. He seemed overly interested in hearing the details. Sometimes he would bring a young man with him and he would watch the whore service his "guest." Later, it was clear to the girls that Del Monte's interest was with boys and young men.

At first when we really did not know him, Caravaggio and I decided it was best to keep me hidden. With time, it was obvious that I was more than welcome. In fact, Del Monte liked lots of boys around him, and Caravaggio introduced me as his model. Of course, the Cardinal caught on quickly. He was delighted with my cherubic looks and welcomed me into his household. I sensed I would be seeing much of him, and I did. I think he liked me from the beginning, and I grew to be very fond of the old man.

CARDINAL DEL MONTE

Del Monte was about 50 when we met. Poor fellow, I must say that the rich life of a cardinal did not do much for his health. He seemed very old and fat, although he did live to be 78. Happily and quickly, we moved into his huge palace, the Palazzo Madama, the old De Medici palace only steps away from the Piazza Navona.

One time, I asked the Cardinal why the *palazzo* carried this unusual name. He said that it was built nearly 100 years ago and became the Roman residence for members of the Florentine Medici family. When it became the home of the dowager duchess of Florence, the illegitimate daughter of Emperor Charles V and widow of Alessandro de' Medici, it began to be known as the Palazzo Madama.

It was an enormously grand palace, and we were given rooms in the servants' area, the best rooms either of us had ever had. I had no idea that life could be that easy. Del Monte even arranged a studio for Caravaggio. It was in this studio that I began my career as a model and painter. I also became friends with many of Del Monte's retainers and servants and his noble friends' retainers and servants. Many of those friendships continued throughout my life, and they became valuable contacts and sources of information about the inner workings of some of the most important people in Caravaggio's life.

THE MAN WHO KILLED CARAVAGGIO

The studio was a gigantic room. It proved perfect for some of the large *istoria* paintings that Caravaggio would be called upon to make. Pulleys and ropes could be attached to its high ceiling so that the models could hang from it as angels. I cannot tell you how many hours I spent in uncomfortable slings attached to that ceiling. I must say, though, that being able to attach a sling to the ceiling was helpful when one had to hold a sword or hatchet high above one's head tortuous hour after tortuous hour. We all learned that when you posed for Caravaggio, the only rest would come when he was spent.

Not far away from the Palazzo Madama, separated by open fields and gardens, was the Palazzo Firenze. I am not sure if this palace also belonged to the De Medici family or if it were owned by Del Monte. I do know that the ceiling decorations contained many heraldic shields with the Del Monte coat-of-arms. Mostly Caravaggio painted in the Madama, but we spent a lot of time in the Firenze. The Palazzo Firenze household staff members were quite intolerant of us, and we enjoyed taunting them.

We frequently invited our friends to the Firenze, and more times than I care to admit we would end up in various kinds of orgies. Before long it was clear that Del Monte wanted to be a part of the fun.

CARDINAL DEL MONTE

I mentioned before that in a casino not far away owned by Del Monte, Caravaggio painted an oil-on-plaster ceiling, *Jupiter, Neptune, and Pluto*. It is a gigantic work in concept and execution, and as far as I know it is his only fresco painting. One time while he was laboring on it, flashing a devilish grin, he said, "Wait until you see Neptune. A very important part that you know very well is autobiographical." He added teasingly, "My *cazzo*—Del Monte loves it." He also slyly mentioned that the face of Pluto was a self-portrait. Unfortunately, I never saw the work.

As I mentioned, Del Monte loved to join in our raunchy orgies. He adored rough trade with bonding and the whole bit, and Caravaggio and I had many young friends from the street who were more than happy to "join the party."

But, there was another side to Del Monte. At times he would take me into his private quarters and ask me to cradle him as he murmured "Mama." You can see something of that in an early Caravaggio painting of Saint Francis requested by Del Monte. The fact that Francesco was Del Monte's first name is no accident. A very young-looking Del Monte is Saint Francis in blissful sleep, and I, the holding angel. He is sleeping like a baby in my arms. Del Monte designed the pose, spending hours cradled in my arms while Caravaggio painted. The painting became somewhat famous and is known as *Saint Francis in Ecstasy.*

I fear I am being overly hard on the old man because Del Monte's interest in Caravaggio was strong. I think Del Monte truly loved Caravaggio and I think in some ways me.

Beyond his love, there was another side to the relationship that bothered me terribly. I always felt that Del Monte's masochism compelled him to take the abuse that Caravaggio endlessly heaped upon him and that Caravaggio took advantage of it. At times I suspected that Del Monte's masochism provoked Caravaggio's sadistic treatment of him. As I look back on it, I can hardly believe what Caravaggio put Del Monte through and how the old man time after time protected him. Repeatedly, Del Monte risked his position and reputation to save Caravaggio.

I do not want to underrate this complex man. The *palazzo* held some of the most important intellectual salons in Rome. Caravaggio and I were exposed to many great scientists, philosophers, and musicians and much great thought. Unfortunately, we were more interested in our hooligan friends and whores than in the refinements that Del Monte offered. But even in my youthful ignorance, I was impressed to know that Del Monte was a supporter of the great Galilei Galileo, and I think I even saw him once in the *palazzo.* I know I saw a telescope that I was told Galileo had given this complicated old man.

It was also said that although Del Monte kept his homosexuality a secret, it was enough known that it ended any chance of his being pope. This was confusing to me in that overt homosexuality did not seem to have been a problem for His Holiness Julius III, according to still circulating rumors.

Everyone knew the story of the so-called "monkey boy" and Julius III, then Cardinal Maria del Monte. Scarcely fifty years ago, a 14-year-old street urchin, the *bastardo* of a female beggar, was picked up on the streets of Parma by Cardinal Maria del Monte. The boy was "adopted" by the Cardinal's brother, Baldovino Ciocchi del Monte, so that the boy might continue as the Cardinal's boy-lover. Apparently Cardinal Maria del Monte also liked rough trade because the boy, unruly, foul-mouthed, and raucous, was known as the "monkey boy." In 1550 when the Cardinal was elevated as Pope Julius III, he made the monkey boy, then 17, Cardinal Innocenzo del Monte. After the "monkey cardinal," as he was contemptuously known, was given several positions that he could not handle, he was semi-retired with the title Cardinal Nephew. Julius died in 1555, and Innocenzo continued to cause trouble for subsequent popes and the Church until he died in Rome some twenty years later. I am not sure of the relationship between Maria del Monte and our Cardinal del Monte, but it seems that something strange ran in that family.

One of my first jobs after we were entrenched in the Palazzo Madama was to pose for paintings suggested by Del Monte. One came about in a curious way. The Cardinal wanted a painting for his music room, and Caravaggio obliged by suggesting a group of musicians, beautiful almost spiritual women strumming instruments. Del Monte replied that he envisioned a group of young boys and said that I would be perfect in it. I think Del Monte encouraged Caravaggio to center me in the painting. As it turned out, I am in it twice. A boy off the street whose name I do not remember also appears twice.

Del Monte often visited the sitting room when we were both there. It was clear that he liked to watch us dress and undress. The placement, of course, was Caravaggio's, and Caravaggio added the arrows of the Cupid and the grapes to give the picture a lustful quality. I was pleased that I am twice full faced. The other boy objected mightily that he was present minimally.

The Concert was quickly followed by a beautiful painting of me, *The Lute Player*. Sensuous and sedate, it allowed Caravaggio to do beautiful renditions of musical instruments, a lovely still life, and even calligraphy.

CARDINAL DEL MONTE

In another painting that I rather liked, I seductively slightly bare one shoulder and hold a basket of fruit. Caravaggio's days with D'Arpino paid off. A version of the beautiful still life that Caravaggio did early for Del Monte, which Del Monte gave to a cardinal in Milan, appears in the painting with me. I must admit that that painting made Caravaggio and me famous.

I was less thrilled with *The Bacchus,* also suggested by Del Monte. I think he got the idea for the hair from Japanese woodcuts of geisha girls that were being talked about in art circles. Del Monte deftly posed me. There I am as Bacchus, a very full Bacchus with a bared shoulder and one nipple showing. The strong "come on" look with the dropped eyes that I learned from my now previous profession serves the painting well. What a different Bacchus this is from D'Arpino's stolen *Il Bacchino Malato.*

Del Monte came to many of the posing sessions and one time put on the wig that had been fashioned for me and dropped his shirt seductively. We did have to humor him, poor old man, in a variety of ways.

Caravaggio always painted rapidly and assuredly. He did a lot of over-painting and rarely scraped off what he didn't like. *The Bacchus* and *The Boy with a Basket of Fruit* were followed quickly by a painting that assured Caravaggio's success, *The Cardsharps.*

THE MAN WHO KILLED CARAVAGGIO

There I am looking innocent while a French fellow hustler (and I might add a great card cheat) Nicolas is indicating my hand to an unsuspecting and somewhat altered version of me. I have no idea what happed to Nicolas, but it cannot be good.

The painting became a huge success. Rather than idealizing life and spiritualizing being that characterized the popular Mannerist style, *The Cardsharps* and another painting called *The Fortuneteller* emphasized human gullibility and foible. Artists and critics alike praised *The Cardsharps.* We did not realize it, but this work and Caravaggio's pretty little gypsy girl thief in *The Fortuneteller* were taking painting into a new direction. Both paintings were several times copied by Caravaggio and many unknown others. There was no question regarding Caravaggio's being the talent of the time.

Another painting that involved me from that heady period should be mentioned, *Boy Bitten by a Lizard*. It is an extraordinary painting. The anguish and fear that Caravaggio puts into my face portends the many anguished souls that are to come from his brush. The still life in the painting is easily recognized as his. In it is an extraordinary water-filled vase with reflections, counter reflections, and altered paths of light.

Actually, the painting that I think looks most like me

during that early Del Monte time is *Saint Francis in Ecstasy,* which I mentioned before. I maintain a nostalgic attachment to the wings in the painting. They are to appear and reappear in Caravaggio paintings. I sadly noticed that they were listed in the inventory of the things left in the house in which Caravaggio was living when he had to flee Rome.

In looking back at his paintings of me, I notice that Caravaggio at times gave me heavy eyelids, eyelids characteristic of him. That look seemed to increase with time, especially as we neared the end of our relationship. I have often wondered what it meant that he made me look more like him as our relationship was beginning to unwind. It was as though in his mind he were becoming I and I were becoming he. I did not understand it, but it made me very uneasy, actually it frightened me. I feared it portended that he was headed toward serious mental disaster.

The great success of the Del Monte paintings and the good life we were living in the *palazzo,* rather than bringing peace and tranquility to our lives, brought an increase in Caravaggio's quarrelsomeness and hot-tempered bitterness. I am not sure how many times he was hauled before magistrates and even jailed for fighting, rock-throwing tantrums, carrying illegal weapons, and a host of provocative behaviors. It seemed that poor Del Monte had a full-time job getting Caravaggio out of trouble and out of jail. I am sure that before Caravaggio, the old man did not even know that the infamous, medieval Tor di Nona prison on the banks of the Tiber existed. However, now Del Monte became a frequent visitor rescuing our mutual friend.

Yet despite the troubles with the law and with himself, Caravaggio's fame continued to soar. Ironically and inadvertently, D'Arpino was to propel Caravaggio into celebrity status.

The situation was curious. Everyone was talking about the importance of His Holiness Clement VIII's 1600 Jubilee. Rome was preparing itself like it had not since the time of Julius II. Everywhere palaces were being built; and public buildings, churches, monastaries, convents, and basilicas were being re-burnished. Public areas and *piazze* were being cleared of rubble, rubbish, and debris in anticipation of the gathering of religious and political ambassadors from the great countries of Europe.

The purposes of the Jubilee were many, but a major one was to demonstrate that Rome was the center of the Holy See. Most of this left me cold except that it meant a lot of work for artists, and I was beginning to have some minor recognition. I now had another profession, I was an artist. Being associated with Caravaggio was no small help.

As it happened, D'Arpino was charged with decorating the Contarelli Chapel in San Luigi dei Francesi, the French national church in Rome. We knew the building well for it was near the Palazzo Madama. I have to say that I never much cared for its facade with its ungainly statues proclaiming French national history. I did take some delight, however, in knowing that Martin Luther stayed there during his trial in the nearby Santa Maria Sopra Minerva. Nonetheless, the San Luigi had some artistic distinction in that Domenichino, Giovanni Baglione, and Francesco Bassano il Giovanni all had work there.

The story was that the French Monsignor Matteo Contarelli had acquired a chapel in the San Luigi some thirty years earlier. The chapel was never decorated, and the monsignor died about ten years ago. Little had been done to the church since. With the coming Jubilee, in the Vatican there was much concern. How would the visiting French delegation react to finding its church in a sorry state?

Contarelli's son, Giacomo, undertook to complete his father's chapel, asking that his father's design be carefully followed. I saw some of the papers. Contarelli was a man who knew what he wanted. His design was very specific. There was to be complete ornamental ceiling decoration, a statue of Saint Matthew and the

Angel by Gerolamo Muziano for the altar, and two wall paintings: a Calling of and a Martyrdom of Saint Matthew. Giacomo commissioned D'Arpino to do all of the painting.

Under the press of the Jubilee, D'Arpino, actually his assistants, decorated the ceiling in his usual mediocre style. The work on the wall murals was interrupted when Clement VIII "requested" that D'Arpino decorate the ceiling of the newly established Room of the Vatican Library. There was no doubt about what would happen. With his ambitious personality, D'Arpino neglected the lesser commission, the Contarelli Chapel, for the grander work.

When it was realized what had happened, near panic ensued. It seemed that the French chapel would be left in shambles. Del Monte, although born in Venice, because of his Bourbon ancestry had extensive French connections. Thankfully for us, his help was eagerly sought by the Vatican, and in an audacious moment he suggested the young Caravaggio be commissioned to complete the chapel.

Although Caravaggio had already achieved fame for his easel work, the idea of his doing pieces of this magnitude for a major church in Rome for the Jubilee audiences was, to say the least, unheard of.

CARDINAL DEL MONTE

Against great opposition, Del Monte persuaded the French delegation to hire Caravaggio for this major commission. On 23 June 1599, Caravaggio signed the contract for *The Calling of Saint Matthew* and *The Martyrdom of Saint Matthew.* I proudly witnessed the signing of my friend's first major commission.

Caravaggio, a host of young painters, and I were ecstatic. Try to imagine our glee, not to mention the glorious recognition that came with taking the commission away from the *cavaliere* (as we all in great disgust called D'Arpino). Yet when our enthusiasm had subsided a bit, suddenly Caravaggio realized what a daunting task he was about to undertake. The wall pieces were by far the largest oil-on-canvas paintings he had ever attempted, and they were to be ready in one year!

I had never seen Caravaggio that agitated. A complete mixture of excitement and excruciating fear, he often sank into utter despair. Frequently I would find him sitting in total darkness mumbling to himself, refusing to eat or drink. This alternated with his running wildly about the studio, his eyes ablaze, shouting, "I am the greatest painter in Christendom!" Overnight, the studio in the Palazzo Madama became a living mad house. It was not hard to recruit models. Caravaggio had dozens of swarthy hoodlum friends who easily could be the Ethiopian tormentors of the Saint. He placed me beside Matthew in *The Calling* because he liked striking contrasts of old and young. As I watched the process unfold, I was spellbound by the intensity with which Caravaggio attacked the canvas. Always the intensity was marked by great precision.

In *The Martyrdom of Saint Matthew*, I am crying in terror. I don't remember who was wielding the sword, but he had a great face and body. As an aside, I am also the angel in the cloud, held for hours in a most uncomfortable sling.

To my and everyone's surprise, Caravaggio carefully complied with the French monsignor's written instructions for decoration of the chapel while still giving expression to his adventurous new style. He enlivened the story while at the same time staying in bounds with the commission. For *The Calling*, Caravaggio chose a street peddler from the *rione* for his Matthew. The incredulous face of the peddler as Matthew seems to ask, "How was it possible that I would be chosen by Jesus?" I think inside the peddler was thinking, "How was it possible that I would be chosen by Caravaggio?"

I was struck by how powerful yet obscure Jesus is. Marked only by a faint halo, Jesus's command "Follow me" is in his finger. How like Jesus's finger is Caravaggio's brush. Magic appears wherever it touched. It was utter alchemy. The same magical finger raised Lazarus from the dead in a painting I helped him get a commission for years later in Messina.

Although in *The Calling* there is a window, the light is from above and beyond, truly a spiritual light. Unselfconsciously, Caravaggio contrasts light and dark. This contrast sharply increases in *The Martyrdom*. Caravaggio's stark contrasts instantly became famous and known as *chiaroscuro*. Those who subsequently painted in his style were known as *caravaggisti*.

Modeling for him and watching him paint increased my confidence to pursue painting as a career. Feeling that I understood how he painted showed me the way toward my own work. His painting became the command "Follow me" from him to me.

When the Contarelli Chapel paintings were completed, it seemed that instantly all Rome heard about them and the new young great artist. Lines of people from all walks of life formed around the block to see them. Soon under severe attack from critics and artists, the church fathers realized that Muziano's altar statue of Saint Matthew and the Angel was a mistake, and the church fathers commissioned a new piece by the Flemish sculptor Cobaert.

The Cobaert piece also was rejected, and the French delegation came to Caravaggio for the altar piece. What a triumph! Quickly Caravaggio painted a glorious Matthew hearing the angel whisper to him the gospel. But can you imagine? It was rejected by the church fathers because the feet of the "old boozer" were dirty and his legs were bare. How could a priest possibly perform the miracle of the Eucharist so close to such dirty feet? I think they thought Jesus and the disciples all had clean feet. Lucky for Jesus and his disciples who did not have to deal with the Council of Trent's forty-years-old imposed restrictions on art. Not so lucky for us poor artists.

Not one easily to concede, Caravaggio painted a second, I think less dynamic, Matthew. I noticed that he got back at the fathers by giving them a rather lusty angel with dirty finger nails.

I might add that it took no time at all for the Marchese Vincenzo Guistiniani, a friend and neighbor of Del Monte and the brother of Cardinal Benedetto Guistiniani, to move in and buy the first glorious *Saint Matthew and the Angel*. That prize he got for next to nothing, but he deserved it. What a discriminating eye he had, and what good fortune that was for us. With backing from Del Monte and now Marchese Vincenzo and Cardinal Benedetto Guistiniani, scions of an incredibly wealthy banker, we knew that we were traveling in agreeably heady circles.

The Contarelli Chapel paintings brought to Caravaggio acknowledgement from artists and critics and fame beyond our expectations. And with the fame came much envy and enmity from established artists, especially D'Arpino.

In Caravaggio and my relationships, I felt an increasing distance. I knew from the beginning that the kind of relationship we shared would eventually end. Also, I was getting much less interested in the wild life of the *rione,* while Caravaggio was even more involved in brawling and fighting and more frequently in serious legal troubles.

I noticed also Caravaggio's increasing interest in another Navona *puttano,* the 12-year-old Francesco Boneri. Rumor had it that Cecco, as we called him, was older than 12 and that he shaved his pubic and underarm hair to make himself look younger. However old he was, I was now 22 and that spelled an end or at least a major change in my relationship with Caravaggio. In truth, I was getting a little tired of being his *puttano.*

Caravaggio's relationship with Cardinal Del Monte was changing as well. Although Del Monte remained ever loyal, Caravaggio treated the old man ever worse. Del Monte's close friend, the Marchese Ciriaco Mattei, began actively collecting the new shining star. Caravaggio did several exciting pieces for the Marchese, including *The Betrayal of Christ* about which I have a confession that I will tell you later.

THE MAN WHO KILLED CARAVAGGIO

Before long Caravaggio moved into the Palazzo Mattei, I am sure much to Del Monte's relief. Characteristically, Caravaggio did not tell me about the move, only that he was leaving the Madama. It was clear that I was not going with him and that wherever he was going, Cecco was going too. It was obvious to all that Cecco was his new delight.

Of course, I was sorry to leave the Madama and much envied Cecco living in the Palazzo Mattei. I often passed it and admired its grand foyer. By this time, I well knew the benefits that come with being in good favor with the rich and powerful. Yet, I was eager to try to live by myself and make my own way as a painter. I was pleased that Caravaggio and I were parting friends, and he gave me many assurances that he would occasionally use me as a model and as an assistant.

I found myself a small room above a barrel maker's shop on the Vicolo di Leopardo in Trastevere just across the Ponto Sisto. It was an area where many artists and craftsmen lived and worked. I was excited to know that the Divine Michelangelo had once lived and worked nearby. The room was not far from the Santa Maria della Scala where I heard Caravaggio was being considered for a major commission. I thought it likely that he would ask me to help him with it. The commission for the Santa Maria della Scala was later to be one of his many ill-fated projects. The Trastevere had its night life and its excitement, but it was a far cry from my old *rione*.

Fortunately, I found enough work as an artist so that I could stop hustling—I was too old for it. I did occasionally model for Caravaggio, and he often hired me as an assistant. However, it would give the wrong impression to say that our friendship continued. The word "friendship" was not something that much applied to Caravaggio, even though he did maintain a kind of loyalty to his friends, including me.

Although Caravaggio was traveling in the highest circles, he never gave up the street life, if anything it increased. We often met at taverns and on the street. Of course, I heard a great deal about him from artists, models, friends, and the servants of the great. Caravaggio was in fact the talk of the town.

Caravaggio, *Victorious Cupid*, 1602

Chapter Three

Cecco

On finishing the Contarelli Chapel, again through Del Monte, Caravaggio received another major commission. Tiberio Cerasi, a rich Roman financier, was decorating his new chapel in the Santa Maria del Popolo. Cerasi had commissioned Annibale Carracci, a noted painter and probably the most talented member of the acclaimed Carracci painting family, to do the altar piece.

Carracci had been brought from Bologna by Cardinal Farnese to decorate the ceiling of the Great Gallery of the Palazzo Farnese. This was a major commission as the Palazzo Farnese was considered the grandest of all the *palazzi* in Rome. Adding to its grandeur was the fact that the Divine Michelangelo had provided the design for the remodel of the upper floors.

Carracci was a strange man who progressively got stranger. He seemed to be in another world. He was unkempt, inordinately shy, and known to be violently jealous of other artists. Although he was worshiped by his students, no one else liked him. He was to become estranged even from his painter brother Agostino

Carracci.

Carracci completed the Farnese ceiling in 1601, and the Cardinal was not pleased with its decoration. Carracci fell into a deep melancholy and was inconsolable. He went around Rome saying that that he would never paint again.

I saw the Great Gallery's ceiling several times. Although I admired Carracci's technical skill and wished I had his mastery of fresco painting, indeed the narrative was confused and the ceiling contained too many direct "quotations" from Michelangelo's Sistine Ceiling.

During the depth of his depression, the nearly unhinged Carracci began the altar piece of the Cesari Chapel. Caravaggio was to paint the two flanking pieces, a Saul conversion and a crucifixion of Saint Peter. Each painting was to be about the same size as the Matthew murals in the San Luigi.

I cannot imagine who thought these two could work together. Carracci, only seven years Caravaggio's senior, was an arch critic of Caravaggio and the new realistic style. Further, Caravaggio was now known as *egregius in Urbe Pictor*, the outstanding painter of the city, and Carracci was suffering the Farnese disgrace.

Caravaggio was so excited to receive the commission

that he was unapproachable. Audaciously, he lorded his success over everyone. He pranced around town buying expensive and elaborately decorated clothes. I did not notice much improvement, however, in his personal hygiene.

Caravaggio always had the peculiar habit of wearing clothes until they were rags. When we were younger, I thought it was because we were poor, but when I saw that he did this with his fine clothes, I began to realize that it was more than that. One time he casually mentioned that he knew that the Divine Michelangelo never changed his clothes; that when he died, they had to cut off his boots because they were almost part of his skin. I worried that our Michelangelo Merisi took his name too literally—thinking himself the Divine Michelangelo reincarnate. Of course, I never mentioned this to Caravaggio. Nevertheless, it was only one of many things that caused me to worry about his mental stability.

Although he and Cecco were ensconced in the Palazzo Mattei, a vast complex near the Teatro di Marcello, Caravaggio continued to use the studio in the Madama. I was pleased that he hired me to help with the Popolo commission.

Again the studio was chaotic. There were many hanging slings on pulleys for the models because the poses were hard to hold and, of course, Caravaggio was tireless.

THE MAN WHO KILLED CARAVAGGIO

In *The Crucifixion of Peter,* the crucifiers face away, fully absorbed in the task of raising the cross. The light is on Peter's upper torso and his slightly turned face. Peter, inverted according to tradition, looks to the side. His eyes are filled with anguish and fear. He seems perplexed and searching for meaning in the events. His body, the cross, the lifting men, and the sinews are a study in tension.

The Popolo murals, like Caravaggio himself, were dramatically light and dark. Both were *chiaroscuro:* The light was not a bright, natural light but a mysterious inner glow; the darkness, like the darkness of night, was full of menace, dread, and fear. As a premonition, I knew that his life, a life driven by violence, would be tragic and short.

During the work on the mural, I came to sense how Caravaggio used dramatic diagonals to evoke a feeling of tension and unease as though something menacing were impending. As I watched *The Crucifixion* evolve, I realized that the diagonals Caravaggio painted mirrored his intense internal tensions. Even when he was riding the crest of fame, every move, every utterance, and every brushstroke revealed his barely controlled inner fury. Like his diagonals, Caravaggio's very being seemed destined to come crashing down.

CECCO

At 22, I was beginning to see into Caravaggio and I was beginning to see into myself. Watching him I was learning about myself. Watching him paint, I was mastering techniques and gaining confidence that I was a good artist. I felt indeed I was a painter and was delighted now to have only one profession. But, I could see that neither I nor anyone else would ever attain the brilliant spark that resided within Caravaggio. I knew that he was forging new art and a new way of looking at the realities of life. Even at 22, I knew that I and art owed Caravaggio an immeasurable debt of gratitude.

The work for the Popolo Chapel proceeded at a rapid pace. While working on *The Conversion,* a horse was brought into the studio. The horse began stamping around. As the retainer tried to restrain the horse, quickly Caravaggio took out his brush and rushed to the large wood panel. An ancient red-bearded Saul, with his hands shielding his eyes from the blinding light above, quickly appeared lying on the ground amidst a primal forest of trampling horse and human legs. I, somewhat idealized with reddened hair, as an angel restrain and hold the beckoning Jesus. I must say that an old boozer from the Piazza Navona made a great indignant and beleaguered Peter.

Despite its extraordinary power, Caravaggio knew that

the painting had to be simplified. He quickly turned to begin a second piece of similar size. Not constrained by scripture, in the new painting a young Saul lying on the ground appeared on the canvas. Guided by an elderly attendant, the horse with only a raised foreleg moves gracefully from the boy. In an ineffable gesture of acceptance and submission, the boy's outstretched arms reach toward a spiritual light from above.

By the end of the day, the tension in the studio was almost unbearable. We were completely exhausted but filled with wonderment at what had been achieved. The second painting, a masterpiece, was perfect for the Popolo. I must add that I was a little miffed that Caravaggio did not ask me to be the young Saul in the second version.

Adding to our problems, cheeky Cecco was constantly underfoot in the studio. I had to admire his pluck for he took no guff from Caravaggio, but he was a real *merda*. At times he ridiculed Caravaggio and impudently sassed him. I could hardly believe that Caravaggio would take it until I realized that I had made a big mistake in being as docile with Caravaggio as I had been. We all knew of Caravaggio's urge to hurt and torment. It was a revelation to see that there was a part of Caravaggio that liked being hurt and tormented. I think we can see that complexity in hurting and being hurt later in his great flagellation pieces. With torture, there is almost serenity in Jesus's face.

According to the commission, Carracci's *The Assumption of the Virgin* occupied the exalted altar of the chapel. Caravaggio's *The Crucifixion* and *The Conversion* were side murals.

With the formal unveiling of the Cesari Chapel, the talk was all about Caravaggio's murals. Their physical immediacy, mystery, and innovation intensified the conventionality of Carracci's piece, a crowded *Assumption of the Virgin* stifled by the rigid moral standards of the Church.

Critique of Carracci's work was loud and sustained. He did not take the negative criticism lightly and fought back. Strangely, he criticized Caravaggio for using live models. Further, he alleged that the reason Caravaggio did not draw on the canvas was because Caravaggio could not draw. He accused Caravaggio of being given to dramatization rather than revealing depth.

To some extent Carracci was correct, especially about the dramatization. But, Carracci could not realize that Caravaggio was forging a new kind of art. What he did realize was that Caravaggio was making him and his kind of art obsolete. In the end, Carracci was to be added to the ever-growing list of envious artists who disliked Caravaggio and who were all too eager to destroy him.

THE MAN WHO KILLED CARAVAGGIO

Fully part of the Palazzo Mattei, Caravaggio finally gave up his studio in the Palazzo Madama. I never knew why Caravaggio left the Palazzo Madama. Truly Del Monte had more than enough reason to be fed up with him, but I do not think that was the cause. In fact, throughout Caravaggio's life Del Monte remained the faithful friend who time and time again came to Caravaggio's rescue often at his own peril.

I think Caravaggio's moving may have had something to do with political reactions to his style of painting. Cardinal Girolamo Mattei was an acknowledged pillar of the Council of Trent reforms. Paradoxically, his influence as a conservative leader of the Church may have provided a better shield for the radical Caravaggio than Del Monte. Del Monte's influence was always somewhat fragile because of his Francophile leanings. Also, increasing revelations of Del Monte's homosexuality may have been a growing concern, even though homosexuality was rampant in the Church. It is hard to imagine how hypocrisy riddled those times. I can remember a learned cardinal discussing that sexual exploitation of boys was within the Judeo-Christian tradition because boys were neither women nor men.

Although the real story behind the move will forever remain hidden to me, I do know that there was a lot to be afraid of in being associated with Caravaggio. His art constantly pressed the limits, especially the Council of Trent restrictions. We all vividly had in mind that the radical philosopher Giordano Bruno was burned as an heretic in the Campo de' Fiori the year of the Jubilee, 1600!

Nevertheless and despite the conservatism of the Church and its affect on art, Caravaggio's fame continued to rocket skyward. Everyone wanted a piece by him, including a growing number of wealthy merchants who like the noble families wanted to decorate their homes with art. Private commissions abounded, and private commissions meant less restraint. We artists took the opportunity to enjoy the freedom and were eager to cash in on the ever-increasing market.

Following the move to the Palazzo Mattei, Caravaggio produced a series of marvelous easel paintings. As much as I disliked Cecco, his pose in *The Sacrifice of Isaac* was perfect. It was astonishing how he could hold the look of a frightened, anguished boy for hours. He tried to convince us that he posed for both angels, but that is hard to see. I like to think that the stranglehold Abraham has on Isaac is Caravaggio's wish at times to throttle that little *stronzo*.

The Sacrifice is without doubt a powerful painting and was much appreciated by Cardinal Maffeo Barberini who commissioned it. Strangely in the background is a soft landscape, something unique in Caravaggio's work. I cannot help but think that he was getting back at Carracci for Carracci's criticism of the Popolo murals. It must be remembered that Carracci at the time was highly admired for his landscape backgrounds.

Caravaggio created many copies of these easel paintings, as did numerous other painters. He hired me to work on some. I cannot tell you how many times we copied *The Supper at Emmaus.*

The Supper was commissioned by Ciriaco Mattei, Cardinal Mattei's brother, and was an early piece for the Mattei collection. In the painting, Jesus is more Mannerist than was characteristic for Caravaggio. He is clean-shaven with a very full and unattractive face. The lighting is bright, and one of the figures at the supper wears a shell of Saint Jacques on his jerkin. Why is Jacques there? Except for the table decorations, the work is largely free of any noteworthy Caravaggio brilliance. Central in the painting is the luscious fruit with the characteristic leaf hanging over the edge of the basket reminiscent of the early still life now proudly displayed in Milan by Archbishop Cardinal Borromeo.

I always thought *The Supper* confused and unappealing. It is perhaps my least favorite of all of Caravaggio's work, although it was widely popular.

CECCO

Ironically, Caravaggio was later to paint another and more brilliant version of *The Supper at Emmaus* under the most extraordinary of circumstances. While on the lam, pursued by powerful enemies, and fearful for his life, Caravaggio took refuge north of Naples in Zagarolo on an estate owned by the Marchesa Colonna. The Zagarolo *Supper at Emmaus* is full-force Caravaggio. An un-haloed Jesus is half-lighted, and his powerful pointing index finger creates the drama. The onlookers are poor, aged, worn, and intently contemplative. Slight white wrappings highlight their heads, lifting the viewers' eyes upward. The bread to be blessed is simple and dry. The top of the table reveals an elaborate but ancient frieze that links the time to antiquity. The painting demonstrates that as Caravaggio's life intensified, so did his ability to paint the miracle of the hope for salvation.

Among my favorite pieces to burst from Caravaggio's easel during his time at the Palazzo Mattei were *The Doubting Thomas* and *The Taking of Christ.* It is incredible how Caravaggio was able to crowd figures and yet keep the focus on dramatic action. In *The Doubting Thomas,* Caravaggio's symbolic use of realism is rarely equaled. Jesus's stigmatized left hand steadies and guides Thomas's hand as Thomas's probing finger disappears into the wound of the "Word Made Flesh" erasing all doubt that Jesus surmounted death. In *The Taking of Christ*, I believe the face of Jesus is one of Caravaggio's most beautiful portraits.

The original version of *The Supper at Emmaus, The Doubting Thomas*, and *The Taking of Christ* were all much copied by us and others. It was only later that I realized what a mistake it was that we produced copies. At the time the situation was heady. All we thought was that people wanted the paintings.

I did have my secret revenge against all the greats who past and future greedily sought Caravaggio's art. I am not proud of this, but I will mention it as I am old and there is little time left. When Caravaggio did the glorious *The Taking of Christ*, I helped him with it. On completion, I delivered it personally to Ciriaco Mattei. My confession is that the painting I delivered was a copy that I made. In the original, the onlooker with the lantern on the far right is Caravaggio's self-portrait, somewhat idealized and more handsome than he was. In my copy, I made the onlooker look more like me.

I hid the original painting thinking that it was just payment for all the abuse I had taken. I lived in fear that Caravaggio would discover the switch, but he never did. Not too long later, I sold the original to Peter Rubens, a young Flemish artist and art dealer, who promised to get it out of the country by attributing it to Gherardo delle Notti, the Flemish *caravaggista*. I think Gherardo's real name was Honthorst. I often wonder about the fate of the real work but take some delight in the fact that my copy passed as an original.

Incidentally, I caution anyone regarding the Caravaggio oeuvre. There are many copies and purposeful fakes being sold as the real thing. Actually, I always suspected that Rubens made a copy or two of some of the paintings.

Also for Ciriaco Mattei, and for obvious reasons I was not a part of it, Caravaggio did a sensuous *Saint John the Baptist* caressing a ram's skull for which Cecco only too gladly posed naked. Here, Cecco's nakedness was modest, however, compared to the yet-to-come full frontal *The Victorious Cupid* on used bed linen for the Marchese Vincenzo Giustiniani. In *The Victorious Cupid*, the little *merda* added insult to (my) injury by wearing my angel wings. My, how much he loved showing off his tiny *cazzo*.

I must admit that a year or so later, Cecco posed for a second and very beautiful *Saint John the Baptist*. In this painting, Cecco, his nakedness covered, looks contemplatively down, holding his staff. John's face is classical, his gentle body musculature defined by a wrapped red cloth, and his feet are intertwined amid primordial plants. All are lighted from above. The background is perfectly muted. The Genoese Ottavio Costa instantly recognized that he had a masterpiece and asked us to make a copy.

It was galling to hear Cecco say that Caravaggio was teaching him to paint because Caravaggio let him fill in space and shadows. He boasted that someday he would be as great a painter as Caravaggio. He strutted around saying that he would be Cecco da Caravaggio, Cecco from Caravaggio, like the master. We said he would be Cecco di Caravaggio, Cecco of Caravaggio.

Cecco did seem to have a talent for painting dripping blood, and he eventually made a career as a painter, albeit a limited one. His paintings became known for their depiction of brutality. I think he learned much from Caravaggio's early decapitation painting of *Judith Beheading Holofernes,* a curious painting. Judith, our beautiful prostitute friend, Annuccia, is repulsed by the disgusting task she has been given as she pulls Holofernes's head back by the hair and blood spurts forth from her slicing sword. Cecco claimed that he did the blood, but I doubt it. The painting, although strong, seems stilted compared to later Caravaggio decapitation paintings when his painting was acutely informed by the anguish and horror that came from his personal acquaintance with this hideous death.

During this time, Caravaggio also produced an extraordinary easel painting, *The Victorious Cupid,* commissioned by the Marchese Vincenzo Guistiniani. Based on the famous line,

"Love conquers all, let us all yield to love" from Virgil's *Ecologues,* the painting was an incredible success. The Marchese said it was derived from Michelangelo's *ignudi* of the Sistine Ceiling and surpassed them. I think he was covering the fact that he liked his boys naked. I even heard that the Marchese kept the painting covered with a dark green silk because it increased the drama to stand before it and have it suddenly undraped. I think the Marchese was vicariously stripping our little *cazzo* naked.

The Victorious Cupid became a *cause célèbre,* and like so many things that should have caused good fortune, it caused Caravaggio great grief. The Cardinal Benedetto Giustiniani, Vincenzo's brother, out of jealousy for his brother's famous painting, commissioned Giovanni Baglione also to create a painting based on the same famous line of Virgil's poem.

Baglione, only five years older than Caravaggio, was a highly regarded painter. Already he was a favorite with the Church hierarchy and in 1607 was knighted by His Holiness Paul V. Baglione's style was Mannerist and only tended to verge on the new realism. Many said that he was influenced by Caravaggio, although he would be the last to admit it.

For reasons I do not know, Baglione did two rather sloppy paintings both called *Divine Love Overcoming the World, the Flesh, and the Devil*, in competition with Caravaggio's widely lauded painting. One version has the devil's back toward the viewer. In the second, the devil is facing the viewer. It is easy to see that the devil is Caravaggio. Even though Caravaggio was dour, ill tempered, and arrogant, everyone knew that he did not deserve that kind of ridicule. Baglione's two paintings were both unfavorably compared with Caravaggio's vibrant *The Victorious Cupid* by critics, artists, and the public at large.

When it came to jealousy, if D'Arpino were bad Baglione was worse. Caravaggio with his fame and great talent was the ready victim of their intense jealousy. As one young painter said of Baglione, "If envy is one of the seven deadly sins, we know who the devil is in the painting." The problem with Baglione was to escalate.

Baglione was commissioned to paint a large altar piece for the Gesù Church, a commission Caravaggio longed for. The Gesù painting, an immense *The Resurrection of Christ*, was unveiled Easter Sunday, 1603. Mind you, Caravaggio had not long before painted the stunning and highly acclaimed *The Entombment*.

Girolamo Vittrice commissioned *The Entombment* as the altar piece for his uncle's chapel in the Oratorian Chiesa Nuova. Consecrated in 1599, the Chiesa Nuova rests on the site of the old

CECCO

Santa Maria Vallicello.

The Congregation of the Oratory was founded by Filipo de Neri, a rather joyous priest who became known as the "Apostle of Rome" because of his devotion to the sick and poor. The antithesis of Jesuit autocracy, the Oratorians are a rather independent congregation of priests and lay-brothers who live together in a community bound together by no formal vows but only the bond of charity and devotion to the care of the sick and poor. Although Neri specified that the decoration for his church should be sparse and entirely devoted to the life of the Virgin Mary, *The Entombment,* with its many elements of the new direction Caravaggio was taking art, was much appreciated and admired by the forward-looking Oratorians. In fact, it is one of the rare times that Caravaggio's work was immediately embraced by church fathers.

In *The Entombment,* Caravaggio places the figure of Christ slightly diagonally with his dead weight barely managed by the aged Nicodemus and a young assistant who tenderly supports Jesus's upper body. The grieving mother Mary, her eyes cast downwardly in silent resignation, echoes the attitude of the lovely Magdalene. The horizontal burial slab projects sharply into the foreground, giving a sense of enduring stability. The slab supports Nicodemus's firmly placed feet. His bare legs form an inverted V that repeats the inverted V made by Jesus's legs as they are lovingly gathered by Nicodemus's cradling arms. Because of that painting alone, Caravaggio should have been given the Gesù commission.

I should also make mention that the Oratorians with their "modern" philosophies six years later commissioned Peter Rubens to paint a remarkable Madonna and Child that covers the thirteenth-century icon of the Blessed Virgin that is enshrined above the high altar. He also did two large side panels in oil that show indebtedness to Caravaggio.

Returning to Baglione's *The Resurrection of Christ*, on its completion, all Rome turned out at the Gesù for the unveiling. The painting was widely criticized as conventional and stylistic. Baglione did not take the criticism lightly, and in August 1603 he sued several critical poets, a number of artists, including Orazio Gentileschi, the architect Onorio Longhi, and of course, Caravaggio.

Strangely, Caravaggio's own words, although owning up to his criticism of the painting, as contrasted with his painter and poet friends were marked by an uncharacteristic decorum and carefulness. Caravaggio said, "I don't think there's any painter at all who thinks Giovanni Baglione is a good painter. I have seen almost all his work, most recently *The Resurrection of Christ* at the Gesù. I don't like the painting. It is clumsy, the worst he has done. I have heard no painter speak well of it." These were Caravaggio's words. We all heard them, and they seemed fair to us. Unfortunately, they were widely quoted in the newspapers.

Despite the moderation, to everyone's horror Caravaggio was again placed in the Tor di Nona, this time for slander. I think that the Jesuits joined Baglione in attempting to destroy Caravaggio because of the audacity in his personality and painting. The Jesuits knew that Caravaggio was changing art and feared, rightly so, that the Church was having less and less influence over what the public would be allowed to see. Caravaggio was fast becoming the flashpoint in this enormous and vicious political struggle.

Two weeks later Caravaggio was released through the influence of Del Monte. Yet so great was the influence of Baglione, and I think the Jesuits, that despite the French ambassador's and Del Monte's pressures, Caravaggio on release from prison was placed under house arrest, a great humiliation to the *pictor praestantissimus* of Rome.

Caravaggio was confined to the lower level of a two-story house that belonged to the widow Prudenzia Bruni on the lane of San Biagio near the Campo Marzio. Things really became confused at this point because so much was happening. Although

THE MAN WHO KILLED CARAVAGGIO

Caravaggio had many highly placed supporters and friends, he was developing a horde of vindictive foes, and although flooded with commissions, the humiliation of the house arrest naturally further embittered him. Caravaggio became markedly suspicious about Baglione and the Jesuits. Of course, he was right—they were out to get him. Increasingly, Caravaggio dwelled on the unfairness and sank deeply into gloom.

He continued to paint in the basement rooms of Signora Bruni's house. In some of these paintings, it is easy to see the trapped, cellar feeling that he was experiencing. To everyone's surprise, Cecco stayed with him through all this. To Cecco's credit, I heard that he stayed with Caravaggio through all the travails until Caravaggio fled to Malta.

I was not to hear about Cecco again until many years later when that cheeky boy panned himself off as Cecco da Caravaggio. I know of two major works that he completed, a *Resurrection of Christ*, which I heard was rejected, and a *Guardian Angel with Saints Ursula and Thomas*, which I saw. I must say that the *Guardian Angel with Saints Ursula and Thomas*, although overly hard-lined, is a good painting. Noticeable is Caravaggio's *chiaroscuro*. Unfortunately, as with many who copied Caravaggio, the *chiaroscuro* is overly intensified. Although it adds dramatic effect, it lacks the magical

CECCO

ethereal quality of Caravaggio. Most interesting, I also saw a self-portrait painted when he was about 20. To my astonishment, Cecco had painted himself with Caravaggio's own heavy lidded eyes, eyes that I knew neither he nor I possessed but that Caravaggio progressively painted as mine as our relationship aged.

Caravaggio, *Madonna di Loreto*, 1604-5

Chapter Four

Women and Caravaggio

From everything I knew, Caravaggio was adamantly, openly, and often provocatively homosexual. More than anything else, he enjoyed being with, playing with, fighting with, *scopando*, and *scopando farsi* young boys and young men. Yet there were women in his life, many of whom played important roles, and they could not have been more different. The most important were his mother, a marchesa, and three Roman tarts.

I know nothing about Caravaggio's mother except that she died when he was about 15. He never mentioned her, but there were widespread rumors that there were major family difficulties following her death. Sometimes I got the picture that there was vicious fighting among the siblings over the disbursal of the Caravaggio property in Caravaggio. As mentioned, there was always ugly rumor that Caravaggio had been in jail in Milan. Although it was often said that he was in jail because of a fight and maybe because of a murder, sometimes it was said that he was in jail because he attempted to abscond with family money or did not pay his taxes. As I mentioned previously, a visit shortly after he came to Rome from his younger brother, the priest, ended disastrously. In any case, there were hard feelings among his siblings, and he rarely talked about them or his mother. Yet, I feel Caravaggio was deeply affected by her death. He often called himself an orphan.

The reason I suspect special feelings for his mother is because of a strange experience I had with him when we first met. I had just come to Rome and indeed was a lost soul as was he. He had recently left the studio of D'Arpino.

One time we were in the Piazza Navona talking until early in the morning. We walked over to the Sant'Agnese in Agone and sat on the steps of the great church that dominates the Piazza, admiring the goings-on of the passers-by. Caravaggio was silent and then without warning asked if I knew the story of Saint Agnes and her young friend. Of course, I did not.

With great seriousness, he said, "Saint Agnes was a young girl about 13 from a noble Roman family. She was raised a Christian. I believe her mother was most influential in her being a Christian.

"A Roman prefect wanted her to marry his son, and she refused unless he became a Christian. The prefect was outraged by her audacity and condemned her to death. Roman law did not permit execution of virgins, so the prefect had Agnes dragged naked through the streets to a brothel. As she prayed, her hair grew and covered her body. It was said that all of the men who attempted to rape her were immediately struck blind. She was taken to be burned at the stake in the Piazza Navona, but the bundle of wood would not burn. She was immediately beheaded. Her head is here in the Sant'Agnese. Her body was taken to a Christian catacomb outside the walls of the city.

"A few days later, a 12-year-old girl was found praying at the grave site. She said that she was the daughter of Agnes's wet nurse. The authorities tried to pry her away from the grave, but she refused to leave. She was stoned to death on the spot and her body placed near Agnes's. She is Saint Emerentiana." Caravaggio turned to me and said, "Sometime let's visit their graves."

One sunny day we went out to Sant'Agnese Fuori le Mura beyond Michelangelo's Porta Pia near the mausoleum of Santa Costanza. We found the church that had been built over the catacomb that contained the remains of the two children. It was in terrible condition. Nearby, also in dreadful shape, was the mausoleum. Exploring the mausoleum, we found areas of intact mosaics, enough to be awestruck by the ruin.

We sat on the grass and Caravaggio continued the story of

the saint. "The great emperor Constantine's daughter, Costanza, developed a strange skin disease. In some way she learned of Agnes and visited the site of her execution in the Piazza Navona. She was miraculously cured. She sought out the burial site of Agnes and built the church over the catacomb that held the bodies of the two girls. When Costanza died, she asked that she be buried near the child saint. It is said that she was buried in a great sarcophagus of carved porphyry. I do not know where it is."

The point of the story is that when we visited Saint Agnes's tomb, Caravaggio wept. It was the only time I ever saw him cry. When I asked him, he hesitantly said, "It pains me when I think how young girls are forced to marry. The men are always brutal!" He made a small reference to his mother and sank into a gloomy silence.

It was a side of him that I never saw again. Yet in looking back on his life, I was always struck by how patient, caring, and tender Caravaggio was with the female models. He even seemed to paint differently when he was painting a woman. They emerged on the canvas with the lightest touch. It was as though even on the canvas they could easily be hurt.

Strange as it may seem given the way he lived, Caravaggio was also kind of a prude regarding women. In his many nudes,

WOMEN AND CARAVAGGIO

there is only one female nude, Pero in *The Seven Works of Mercy*. In the painting, she bares only one breast as she nurses her imprisoned and starving father Cimon. I think he thought men sullied the purity in women and was afraid that he might too. This brings to my mind the Divine Michelangelo's *Pietà* in Saint Peter's with the Virgin's pure and unsullied child-like face. The Divine also lost his mother when he was young. I wonder if deeply in Caravaggio there dwelt an identification with women, particularly abused women. I think that his artistic sensitivity and the beautiful and caring way he portrayed women came from this part of him.

A woman who was of vast importance in Caravaggio's life was the Marchesa Costanza Colonna. I never met her, but I occasionally saw her arrive in her carriage at Del Monte's. She lived in the massive Palazzo Colonna that faces the gigantic second-century Column of Marcus Aurelius centered in the Piazza Colonna not far from the Piazza Navona. Of course the famous, powerful, and fantastically rich Colonna family has numerous *palazzi* and estates throughout the length of Italy, and through her family the Marchesa had many important contacts from Genoa to Naples and even in Malta.

Frankly, I have difficulty keeping track of the noble families in that they are completely intermarried. But as far as I know, the

THE MAN WHO KILLED CARAVAGGIO

Marchesa Colonna was the daughter of the great hero Admiral Marcantonio Colonna who was important in defeating the Turks at Lepanto in 1571. As a child, Costanza was married to Francesco Sforza, who carried among his titles the Marchese da Caravaggio. I think that is how she became the Marchesa da Caravaggio. In any case, we always called her the Marchesa Colonna. She was clearly a strong-willed woman, and I'm told not overly attractive. She was well-known as a great patron of the arts and new sciences. It was in their mutual interest in and patronage of the arts and science that she and Cardinal del Monte found their friendship.

I find it uncanny that two marchesas Colonna would be important persons in the lives of two great artists. The Marchesa Vittoria Colonna, known for her poetry and her patronage of the arts and artists, was an important woman in the life of Michelangelo Buonarroti, and some fifty years later the Marchesa Costanza Colonna would be important in the life of Italy's second greatest painter, Michelangelo Mersi.

Noble people have a way of forgetting that servants (and artists) are actually real people, except when they need us. They have a tendency to speak in front of us forgetting that we are there. A servant of Del Monte's once told me he overheard a conversation between the Marchesa and the Cardinal. She spoke of her interest and fondness for Caravaggio. She said that even though he was inordinately difficult, she always felt a kinship to him because of her family's long association with the community of Caravaggio. Even in those early days, she professed to Del Monte a genuine desire to help Caravaggio, indicating that she considered him the greatest living artist.

The Marchesa's loyalty to Caravaggio was enduring. I think it was fuelled by recognition of his great talent but also a genuine concern for those who were subjected to vindictive envy and injustice. Without question, the Marchesa played an important role in Caravaggio's life until its very end.

On the opposite end of the social spectrum, a number of prostitutes were important in both my life and especially in Caravaggio's. During the early time at the Palazzo Madama when Caravaggio was producing wonderful pictures for Del Monte and his friend Vincenzo Giustiniani, without doubt both noblemen loved hearing tales about our hoodlum exploits. I think they vicariously lived the wild street life through us. Yet, it was through them that we met several young street girls who were to become important in our, especially Caravaggio's, lives.

Anna Bianchini, known as Annuccia, and her friend Fillide Melandroni each came from Tuscany when they were 12 and 13.

They arrived in Rome with their mothers and several siblings. Their mothers were prostitutes and set up the most sought after brothels in the *rione* with both girls working for their mothers. Shortly after they came to Rome, Fillide with her beautiful, silken auburn hair quickly became a favorite of Vincenzo. Both Del Monte and Giustiniani thought Annuccia and Fillide would be great models and introduced the girls to Caravaggio and to me. Incidentally, in addition to our artistic relationships and personal friendships, the girls also became a source of much of our information about Giustiniani and other highly placed men.

Annuccia and Fillide were small and beautiful. Make no mistake though in thinking that these were girls who needed to be coddled and protected. They, like all of our friends, were tough street walkers. They lived on the street, lived by its rules, and talked from it.

I had a friend who was at the police station one time when Fillide was hauled in. She had been in a cat fight with another whore, Prudenzia Zacchia. My friend, who was a wonderful mimic, told of their coming into the station all bloodied, clothes torn, and screaming at each other. The police sergeant separated them, and Prudenzia screamed at the clerk, "Fillide came to me with a knife. She went for my face. It was all her fault. I did nothing. I fended her off … she got me about the wrist." Fillide screamed back, "You are a liar! You are nothing but trash. I got you in the hand you lazy *troia*. I wanted to get you in the face, and the next time I will."

Now, doubled over, and almost rolling on the floor with laughter, my friend continued. "Can you believe it? Fillide then went after Prudenzia again, right in the police station! It took several men to separate them. Prudenzia scratched one officer in the face. He laughed and said 'You will pay for this later.' We all snickered because we knew what he meant."

Oh, we all loved the wild side of these girls! Del Monte and Giustiniani even yearned for Caravaggio to paint the beautiful wildcats. Caravaggio complied with a rather standard portrait of Fillide for Giustiniani, however both Annuccia and Fillide appeared in many early and important paintings, Annuccia more so than Fillide. It saddens me when I think about these vivacious free spirits and realize how each of them came to an early death. I must say that the same can also be said for most of our young artist friends.

Annuccia with her lovely auburn hair made the perfect Magdalene. I think Caravaggio's painting of her as *The Penitent Mary Magdalene,* tenderly asleep, her jewels cast aside beside the vessel containing the oil to bathe the dead Jesus, is his most beautiful painting.

I am not sure about this, but I think Fillide posed as the boy for *The Narcissus*. In the painting, the boy is lovely. Even if it were not she, I can attest to the fact that she was in love with her looks. I can also attest to the fact that she was never in the slightest bit interested in me. I was always *il ragazzino*.

Annuncia is Judith in *Judith Beheading Holophernes*. In Caravaggio's hands, even as Judith decapitates Holophernes, she does not seem vicious. Her intense look and furled brow show resolve rather than brutality. Incidentally, I believe this painting wonderfully shows the way Caravaggio likes to pair youth with its promise of the future with the involution of age and its harking to the past. Alongside the lovely and intense Judith, cloth in hand and waiting to receive the fruits of the terrible task, is a crone.

Later Caravaggio again chose Annuccia as the Magdalene in *The Conversion of Mary Magdalene*. In fact, I think Annuccia is both the sister Martha and the Magdalene, although Martha may be Fillide. It is interesting that the pleader Martha is the more arresting portrait, although her hands seem overly Manneristic. Both girls are in *The Entombment of Christ* as minor side figures. Annuccia with head bowed stands in front of a dazed Fillide whose eyes and hands are raised upward.

WOMEN AND CARAVAGGIO

Annuccia makes a lovely *Saint Catherine of Alexandria,* but both this painting as well as *The Conversion of Mary Magdalene* leave me a little cold. In the *Saint Catherine,* Caravaggio relies too heavily on the instruments of Catherine's torture, the spiked wheel and the bloody rapier, and the palms of martyrdom to tell the story. Again, the story is of a young woman, Catherine, who chooses torture over losing her virginity or her faith.

More complex was Caravaggio's tender and close relationship with the somewhat older and more experienced prostitute Maddalena Antognetti, known as Lena. Elegant and stately, the daughter and sister of famous courtesans, she certainly was a favorite of the Church hierarchy. I often wondered why she was not a courtesan.

I fondly remember her. She was always kind to me, called me by name, and took the time to talk with me. Thoughtfully, she often bought me sweets and other tasty morsels to eat.

The situation between Caravaggio and Lena was different from his relationship with other women. She was the one woman for whom I suspect Caravaggio had deep feelings. She could make him laugh and was the only person who could tease him and get away with it. I do not know if they were ever sexually intimate, but I doubt it. However, it was rumored that her child in the famous

THE MAN WHO KILLED CARAVAGGIO

La Madonna dei Pellegrini was Caravaggio's. When asked about it Caravaggio said, "I don't believe in immaculate conception." Actually, the child could not have been his. The child was born before Lena and Caravaggio met.

I am not sure how Lena came into Caravaggio's life. I believe his first encounter with her had to do with the painting of the Holy House of Loreto.

The Holy House, and I am not overly strong in knowledge about these religious stories, is related to a furor that arose in Italy about 150 years ago. It seems that in the eleventh century the house in Nazareth in which Jesus was conceived and raised had by a circuitous route miraculously landed intact in Loreto, a small town near the coast of the Adriatic. I think this had to do with the crusades and the Muslims.

In any case, in the fifteenth century Loreto became a popular pilgrim site, and an enormous basilica was built to protect the Holy House. Many important architects were involved, and I think there are paintings by greats such as Melozzo da Forli and Luca Signorelli. Caravaggio heard that an altar piece was being commissioned for a chapel in the basilica. As expected, the commission was given to a conservative, steady painter. I forget his name, but I think he was a student of the painter Lorenzo Lotto, who died in Loreto.

WOMEN AND CARAVAGGIO

Caravaggio very much wanted the Loreto commission. More accurately, Caravaggio could not stand it when he was not given any commission that ended up with a lesser painter, which included most painters as far as Caravaggio was concerned.

Thankfully, Caravaggio received an important Roman commission during that time. Those of us who knew how Caravaggio dwelt on injustice, which meant any time he was denied something he wanted, were grateful that his temper was temporarily quelled by receiving this new commission.

The family of Ermet Cavaletti, a wealthy banker, wanted a Madonna altar piece for a chapel in the Sant'Agostino, which was located only a few blocks away from the San Luigi dei Francesi and half way toward the Santa Maria del Popolo. (Imagine the line of great Caravaggio art that was about to become.) To show the people of Loreto what they had missed, spitefully Caravaggio produced the incredibly beautiful *La Madonna dei Pellegrini,* also known as *La Madonna di Loreto.*

In Caravaggio's altar piece, the Madonna with a faint halo looking serenely downward is Lena, and what a madonna she is. In the painting, the Virgin is appearing to an elderly couple kneeling in the doorway of the Holy House. The Virgin is barely able to hold the overly large child Jesus. (Caravaggio shows us what a great burden it was to be the mother of a miraculous child.) Her foot, as graceful as the Divine Michelangelo's *Libyca sibyl* in the Sistine Ceiling, lightly touches the thrusting horizontal stoop from which arise intense verticals forming the doorjamb framing her. The verticals and the horizontals give a sense of stability and security to the ineffable tableau. Below are the barefoot peasants—I believe the donors—dirty and worn, but with faces rejuvenated by the vision. To think this transcendental painting came from a man who only shortly before was under house arrest because of slanderous remarks he made about a mediocre Baglione painting.

It is not an exaggeration to say that all Rome crowded the streets to see this latest Caravaggio painting. Nobles, clerics, artists, poets, and critics all wanted to see it. Most touching were the lines of common folk who came to see themselves for the first time in a church painting. To be expected, some of the church fathers were upset. Again, the concern was with the dirty peasants and their dirty feet being too close to the tabernacle of the Holy Eucharist. Fortunately, acclaim overcame silly objection and the painting remained.

As an aside, in the midst of this triumph Caravaggio left Signora Bruni's house. His release from house arrest was once again the result of the skillful intervention by the ever-faithful Del

WOMEN AND CARAVAGGIO

Monte. True to his self-destructive nature, Caravaggio, probably in spite, left the widow without paying her rent and reimbursing her for damage to her house. You see, Caravaggio had made a hole in the ceiling in order to hang an extended upper arm of a model for a large painting. Signora Bruni brought legal action against Caravaggio. It seemed at the time that everyone was bringing legal actions against him, warranted and not warranted. The case was closed when Signora Bruni was awarded the scant possessions Caravaggio had left behind, sadly including the wonderful wings that Cecco and I had many times worn in the early works.

Following the extraordinary success of the altar piece for the Sant'Agostino, Laezio Cherubini commissioned Caravaggio to do a major piece for the new Carmelite church of Santa Maria della Scala in Trastevere. Fortunately, Cherubini gave Caravaggio a free hand. The result was the wonderful and haunting *The Death of the Virgin* in which Lena, pregnant again, is the aging Virgin. With face and hands tinted in grey tones and an abdomen bloated in death, she lies near a grieving Magdalene, our beautiful Annuccia. Free of romantic or spiritual upliftment, it is death as finality.

Of course, such an excellent and innovative rendition would be refused by the church fathers. The theme of the finality of death, particularly the Virgin's, was unacceptable to the Carmelites. Also, the clerics were "appalled" that the models were prostitutes. (I can't help but wonder which of the holy fathers recognized them.)

The painting had an odd history that I learned about later. Peter Rubens, the young Flemish painter and art dealer with whom I had had dealings before, was again in Rome searching for paintings for the Duke of Mantua. Without hesitation, he recognized the value of the painting and secured it for his patron. For some reason, it went to England and later maybe to France. How true it is that a prophet is without honor in his own country. Imagine that wonderful painting forever lost to Italy.

Actually, it was Rubens and later José de Ribera who were among the first from outside Italy to recognize Caravaggio's genius. It is they as ardent followers of his style who carried Caravaggio's fame beyond Italy.

Unfortunately, *The Death of the Virgin* carries with it an ugly rumor. One often hears that the model was a cadaver dredged from the Tiber. It is said that the dead woman was a prostitute. I am sure, however, that Caravaggio's detractors, quick to cast aspersions on him, confuse this painting with *The Resurrection of Lazarus* painted five years later in Messina. In *The Resurrection*, Caravaggio, seriously mentally deranged, did force his models to pose with a corpse.

WOMEN AND CARAVAGGIO

But when Lena heard that the model was a dead prostitute, she was horror-struck, fearing that it portended her own future. Innocently, poor Lena also later became involved in another of Caravaggio's many struggles with the law.

In 1605, a certain Gaspare Albertini, who was in love with Lena and claimed that they were engaged, confronted Caravaggio accusing Lena of being Caravaggio's *troia*. With admirable calm, Caravaggio ignored him. But when in the Piazza Navona Albertini's young upstart lawyer Mariano Pasqualone tried to serve Caravaggio with legal papers, Caravaggio flared up and attacked him with his sword, which he should not have been carrying. Again, Caravaggio was jailed and freed only through interventions of Del Monte, who I think paid off Albertini. The child in *La Madonna di Loreto* and the boy who later appears in *La Madonna dei Palafrenieri* probably was Albertini's. I think Albertini also was the father of the baby Lena was carrying when she posed for *The Death of the Virgin*.

It is easy to lose track of the number of Caravaggio's altercations with the law, but I think between the libel trail and the wounding of the lawyer, Caravaggio was arrested and jailed on at least five separate occasions for brawling, sword carrying, sword fights, rock throwing, and what have you. With the numerous arrests, jailings, the humiliation of the house arrest, and the lack of recognition of his masterpiece *The Death of the Virgin*, it is not surprising that during this sad time Caravaggio painted a sensitive study in maltreatment and abuse by authority, the highly regarded *The Taking of Christ*, his last painting for the Mattei family. I helped him with several rather identical versions of this powerful subject, and as I mentioned, I stole and hid the original.

By this time the Mattei family wanted Caravaggio out of their *palazzo*, and Caravaggio, broke and recovering from a fist fight, moved in with a friend Andrea Ruffetti, a lawyer in the Piazza Colonna. Living with Ruffetti could not last long, however, but while there and desperate for money, Caravaggio accepted a commission from the Papal Grooms for their chapel in Saint Peter's. The Papal Grooms, the *Palafrenieri*, are lay noblemen who attend His Holiness the Pope. Although they paid little, the commission was a great honor and would fulfill Caravaggio's dream of having a painting in Saint Peter's.

The patron saint of the *Palafrenieri* is Saint Anne, and the commission was for a Madonna and Child with Saint Anne. In his *La Madonna dei Palafrenieri*, Caravaggio placed the boy's foot on top of the Virgin's stepping on the serpent in accordance with tradition; however, Anne is an old crone reduced to the role of onlooker.

WOMEN AND CARAVAGGIO

Beautiful Lena as the gentle Virgin, perhaps with a little too much of her voluptuous breasts showing, absolutely sucks your eyes away from her aged mother.

The Grooms were not pleased and rejected the painting. They saw Anne's secondary position in the painting as an insult to their patron saint and objected to the nakedness of Jesus. The placement in Saint Peter's never became an issue because for reasons I do not know the Grooms lost their chapel in Saint Peter's. Caravaggio was deeply disappointed. He realized that he would probably never have a painting in that basilica.

La Madonna dei Palafrenieri found its way into the often dirty hands of Cardinal Scipione Borghese. I have little first-hand knowledge about Scipione Borghese, by which I mean I knew no one in his large household, but I knew a great deal about him from fellow artists.

The Borghese family moved to Rome from Siena, where it had amassed a fortune as wool merchants. The family members established themselves in southern Italy gathering enormous land holdings. In Rome, they lived in a garden estate on the Quirinale.

Scipione came from an impoverished branch of the family, his father being Francisco Caffarelli. His mother, Ortensia, was the sister of Camillo Borghese, who adopted Scipione and gave him the right to use the Borghese name and coat of arms: an eagle over a dragon.

Camillo recognized and fostered Scipione's keen mind and strong ambition. Early on, he assured that his nephew-foster-son was given an excellent education and positions of responsibility and wealth.

Scipione was to gain much power in June 1605 when his uncle-foster-father Camillo was elevated as His Holiness Pope Paul V. In July, at age 28, Scipione was made Cardinal and known as the Cardinal Nephew. The Borghese pope and his nephew were to play a pivotal role in Caravaggio's life, especially in the final days.

By reputation, Scipione Borghese was a man of extreme ambition, completely without scruples. It was well-known that as Cardinal Nephew he often compelled owners to sell their holdings to him at substantial discounts, enormously increasing his family's fortunes.

There was a good deal of secrecy surrounding his personal life, although it was widely thought that he was homosexual. It was known that he had an intensely close friendship with a man one year younger, Stefano Pignatelli, the son of a potter, whom he met in Perugia. Stefano was a connoisseur of art and music, and Scipione brought him to Rome to live with him shortly after his elevation to Cardinal. Over time, Stefano's influence over Scipione was such that a group of highly placed Vatican officials objected to His Holiness, and Pignatelli was made to leave Rome. Scipione took to his bed for many months in utter despair until Stefano was allowed to return. In the way of the Vatican during those days, Stefano was elevated to Cardinal. Can you believe it? He died at age 45 with the whole matter being hushed up.

I must say that Cardinal Borghese's interest in art with homoerotic overtones added to the suspicion. He had a taste for sensual depictions of young male figures. One of his favorite pieces was *The Hermaphrodite,* a beautiful marble that he commissioned from the young Bernini. *The Hermaphrodite,* based on a Roman copy of a Greek original, is a realistically rendered, sensuous nude hermaphrodite reclining on a mattress. I had heard that Borghese kept the statue in a specially made wooden case bringing it out dramatically only to close friends.

Returning to *La Madonna dei Palafrenieri,* we knew that the Cardinal had eyed it while we were working on it. When he heard that the Grooms felt they could not own Caravaggio's art because of the events of 28 May 1606 (a black day for Caravaggio as I will tell you later), the Cardinal thought he could get a bargain and rushed to buy the painting. Everyone knew Borghese had a good eye for art, but we also knew that that he was merciless in his hunt for bargains. In that he especially took advantage of artists, you can imagine how delighted we were to learn, and glory be to them, that the Grooms actually made a profit from Cardinal Borghese.

Attesting to the Cardinal's power and unscrupulousness, to get Cavaliere D'Arpino's excellent art collection, in 1607 Borghese actually had D'Arpino arrested for illegal possession of arms—his gorgeous weapons collection! Guess what the fine was? Really as a bribe, Borghese confiscated many paintings from D'Arpino, including the paintings D'Arpino had taken from Caravaggio when Caravaggio left the apprenticeship in D'Arpino's studio years earlier. That is how Caravaggio's *Il Bacchino Malato* and a host of other works from D'Arpino's excellent collection became part of the growing collection of Cardinal Borghese.

The Boy with a Basket of Fruit has a little different story. Actually, I am "the boy," and it was painted for Del Monte. Why Del Monte gave it to D'Arpino I will never know, but that is how it became part of Borghese's loot stolen from D'Arpino. I do not relate all this because any of us had even an iota of sympathy for D'Arpino, but it seems perverted justice that he lost that precious, but stolen, art.

To further my point about Borghese and art, it is also well-known that a year later Borghese conspired with a highly placed priest in the San Francesco al Prato church in Perugia to "steal" Raphael's famous *Deposition*. To avoid scandal, Borghese's uncle, the Pope, commissioned D'Arpino to make a copy of the painting and the copy was sent to Perugia as placation.

Being an avid collector of art and of Caravaggio's work, the Cardinal set about to promote Caravaggio. He arranged for him to paint a portrait of his uncle, the Pope. I never saw the painting and I do not know any one who did, but I heard from servants that the Pope was outraged by the painting. Caravaggio, the master of realism and unflinching detail, I am sure produced a portrait that the vain old man decided was unflattering and earned Caravaggio the enmity of Pope Paul V. Unfortunately, this was to add immeasurably to the harsh way Caravaggio was treated when he got into really big trouble in Rome, and that was soon to happen.

Caravaggio, *Deposition*, 1602-4

Chapter Five

28 Maggio 1606

Sunday, 28 May 1606, was a day that would change our lives forever. In fact, it was a day that changed art.

But first, I fear that I have been romanticizing Rome and life in Rome. Indeed, I fear that I have given you, my unknown reader, the impression that Rome was a cultivated and civilized city, one largely populated by popes, cardinals, bankers, wealthy merchants, artists, critics, and courtesans.

It is true that at times, especially in the spring, Rome can be glorious with evidences of beauty and grandeur at every corner. Flowers abound among the ancient ruins that rise with majestic, umber-tinted travertine and startling white marble facades. There are many small vales and meadows in which cows and sheep graze, and the ancient fruit orchards on Palatine Hill and the Quirinale are brilliant with their pale pink and white blossoms.

In fact, for most Romans, life centered around the service of the great families and the church hierarchy. These lucky souls lived in the attics, basements, and stables of the grand palaces where they were cooks, bakers, livery men, cleaners, gardeners, care-takers, and nursemaids.

Among the better off were the tavern owners, who lived with their families above their establishments. In most of the taverns, the wives and children worked with the owners, enjoying the good food and wine and the raucous social life of the tavern.

Many Romans were *artigiani,* including potters, vintners, bakers, tinsmiths, carpenters, roofers, and the like. These craftsmen were largely organized into a variety of *sindicati.* Some of the *artigiani* had the good fortune to inhabit crude, dingy, damp homes and apartments with no facilities, often above or behind their *botteghe.* Largely they called the street *la loro casa.*

Children worked with their parents. Some attended religious schools run by nuns. The more fortunate orphans were cared for by various religious groups, but often orphans were used by unscrupulous "adoptive parents" as beggars. Begging was widespread, largely around the religious sites. Here the sick, the blind, and the maimed held out outstretched and diseased limbs to play on the guilt and the superstitions of the innumerable pilgrims who flooded Rome especially on Holy Days.

Pilgrims came from all over Christendom. Some were fabulously wealthy, but most were poor and often ill seeking miracles. Some were housed in hostels run by a variety of religious orders, but most lived on the street or were taken advantage of by innumerable small inns. Of course, there was a huge business in religious chicanery—selling relics and various miraculous items.

Dogs were everywhere and often were ill and mistreated, and since ancient times Rome has been famous for its feral cats, which were considered almost sacred animals. I hate to think of the rat population of Rome if it were not for the efficient efforts of these feline hunters.

For all of Rome, both two-legged and four-legged, life largely took place in the innumerable taverns, in the *piazze,* and on the streets. *Dio mio, le strade!*

The dark crooked streets, the main passage ways of Rome, were jammed with carts, animals, hawkers, and trash. Everywhere people were walking, usually carrying things on their backs or on their heads or pushing carts. Aristocrats, high-level clergy, and wealthy merchants and bankers raced though the streets in covered carriages pulled by teams of horses scattering people left and right.

The twisting alleys were dark and menacing. They reeked from the smell of open sewage and were heaped with garbage thrown down from the windows above.

THE MAN WHO KILLED CARAVAGGIO

Both the main roads and back alleys converged in *le piazze*, big and small. The grand *piazze* were often graced by remarkable fountains provided by our classical ancestors that gave the city blessedly fresh water. But most of the *piazze* were daily choked with market stalls selling produce, meats, and other staples brought in from the countryside on carts or by boat.

The Tiber River, our life line, snaked its way through the heart of the city toward the sea. Trade skiffs of every description plied its waters. The river also served as laundry for the entire city, with clothes left to dry on the banks. The dyers too used the river to catch water in giant basins, and then their newly dyed materials were washed in the flowing waters, tinting the water into curiously beautiful hues. Thankfully, waste was carried downstream, away from our shores.

The police, if you wanted to call them that, were another gang of thugs and thieves. They did not steal outright, but they took bribes, and no one was safe from their rough interrogation. On any pretense they hauled you off to jails, always with their hands out to "make a settlement."

Except for prostitutes and lowly female workers, women were kept at home. It simply was not safe for a woman (or even a man) to walk the streets day or night.

On looking back, I realize how crowded, dirty, and threatening was all of Rome. Yet, we loved it. Even when we were living in the grandest of places, the Palazzo Madama, we could not wait to go out onto the streets, to the Piazza Navona, to the playing fields, and to the taverns. In short, the picture of Rome that I keep in my mind is that of an excitement-seeking, fight-loving, adventurous young man, not the Rome that it was.

Without question, however, I know that I have over-romanticized the *rione* Campo Marzio. Although I loved it dearly, in reality the Campo Marzio was a lawless, rough place, and its playing field was the wildest, roughest place of all. Day and night, aimless and drifting young men milled and drank and engaged in all kinds of athletic contests usually ending in fist fights, rock-throwing battles, general brawling, and riots.

As for Caravaggio, his police record shows his affinity for rock fights, fist fights, sword fights, knifings, and the like. He was always ready for a riot. Never the witness, he quickly joined in any altercation. Rightfully regarded as a hot head, Caravaggio was easily provoked to fight but was also respected for his skillfulness with sword and dagger. He never revealed to me where he learned his weaponry skills, but I know that they were highly intensified by his ever-smoldering anger. Although a seasoned and fierce brawler, I was not skilled with sword or dagger. I too loved a good fight, although I must admit that largely I was but Caravaggio's shadow.

Regarding Caravaggio's temper, one incident stands out in my mind because I was really embarrassed for him. It was late, and several of us were in the Taverna del Moro. Caravaggio ordered a plate of artichokes. The poor young waiter brought them steaming hot, and there was some argument about how they were cooked. Caravaggio ate one and spat it out on the floor, complaining loudly. It really was a trivial complaint, something about whether the artichokes were cooked in olive oil or in butter.

When the waiter tried to explain, Caravaggio, looking for a fight, sarcastically complained, "Can't you tell artichokes cooked in oil from artichokes cooked in butter?" The poor boy stammered, "I don't know" and leaned over to smell them. Without warning, Caravaggio slammed the poor guy's face into the plate breaking his nose. Caravaggio yelled, "You *testa di cazzo*. You think you are serving some two-bit crook!"

I felt intensely sorry for the poor boy. Our friends and I tried to intervene, but Caravaggio continued on a rampage. The police stormed in, and Caravaggio, I, and the innocent young waiter, his face streaming with blood, were hauled off to the police station. We were released with yet another stern warning.

As I look back on those exciting days, I now realize that it was actually a strange and difficult time in Rome, especially for young men. The wars in Eastern Europe had ended disastrously, and there was an unsettled peace with France and Spain. The streets were flooded with adventurers and mercenaries returning from wars. There were many immigrants like me who came to Rome hoping they could find work. Despite the reconstruction, Rome was far from prosperous. Most of the young men were unemployed, and many were unemployable. Added to this there was no shortage of thugs and thieves who wanted nothing more than to roam the streets looking for trouble.

Among this mélange of young men, the Tomassoni boys were always in the thick of the scene. Their family lived in a small *palazzo* near San Lorenzo in Lucina in the *rione*. For generations, the Tomassonis boasted of strong ties to the papacy. They exalted in displaying the many papal honors won in futile religious wars.

Their most recent patriarch, Captain Lucantonio Tomassoni, had died about fifteen years ago. He had been a famous soldier of fortune, or so we were told over and over and over by his sons. Over the years, Lucantonio had become close to the powerful Farnese family. Because of this closeness, Lucantonio named his several sons (I knew at least five) with names long popular with the Farneses. Ranuccio, the youngest, bore one of the Farnese first names. He was about 25 on the fateful day.

Like many young minor aristocrats, the Tomassoni boys had nothing to do. They considered the *rione* their territory, arrogantly parading through the streets and talking about their importance and influence. In fact, it may be that several of the brothers had had distinguished military records, or so we were led to believe, but I doubt that Ranuccio had ever done much in the way of honorable service to anyone. He was, however, married to the sister of an important former military man, Ignazio Guigoli.

Most of Rome knew about the Tomassonis. They were constantly in the taverns and the brothels. They were well-known to the girls of the *rione,* if you know what I mean.

Many times they had appeared before the magistrates because of involvements in brawls, riots, disputes over gaming, and fights over women. Always they were pardoned because of family influence.

Ranuccio had a special liking for Fillide. She and Ranuccio regularly had "carnal relations," as Fillide slyly liked to say. It was rumored that Ranuccio pimped Fillide, which she denied.

In fact, Ranuccio was involved in a number of incidents

with Fillide and several different whores and their clients. He often boasted that he provided "his girls" with protection and was quoted as saying "woe be to any man who hurts or takes advantage of one of *my* girls." I personally knew of several times when Ranuccio was arrested for brick-throwing assaults on men who, so as not to pay for services, were running away from girls Ranuccio was "protecting." Several friends had even told me of being severely beaten by him, even though they were innocent.

Ranuccio's brothers were little better. Everyone disliked them and to some degree feared them. It was known that despite quarreling among themselves, when one was attacked they banded together and fiercely protected each other.

It was destined that Caravaggio and Ranuccio would hate each other instantly. In some ways they were alike. Both were arrogant, hot tempered, easily provoked, and always looking for a fight. Both were excellent swordsmen.

As one would expect when there is a major political-legal situation, there are many versions of what happened on 28 May. The newspaper accounts at the time and subsequently were filled with errors. Some even say the date was 29 May, but I know that it was on a Sunday and that Sunday was 28 May 1606, the first day of the celebration of the anniversary of the coronation of His

Holiness Paul V. Some even called it a "duel" in the playing field of the Campo Marzio. Over the years various versions continued to appear. As Caravaggio's fame increased internationally, the stories reached greater and greater levels of embellishment.

I know what happened because I was there. In fact, over many months there had been a number of threatening confrontations between Ranuccio and Caravaggio, often over trivial matters. Much of the disagreement was about Fillide, about whom Ranuccio was extremely possessive. Ranuccio did not like Fillide's posing for Caravaggio, and he never believed it when she said that Caravaggio was not interested in her sexually. I think that sometimes Fillide tormented Ranuccio on purpose, giving him ideas about Caravaggio and many other men.

On Friday, 26 May, Ranuccio challenged Caravaggio to a handball match in the playing field. I cautioned Caravaggio against entering into it. They already hated each other, and I suspected some sort of a set-up. I should have known better than to say anything. Telling Caravaggio that he should not do something was the same as pushing him into doing it. I was busy at the time and was not present, so I do not know who won nor if Ranuccio's claim that Caravaggio owed him a paltry sum were valid. I certainly can imagine that if Caravaggio did and if Ranuccio pressed him, Caravaggio's response would be as Ranuccio claimed, *"Vaffanculo!"*

Sunday, 28 May, was one of those particularly beautiful Roman days. The sun shone brightly, and all Rome was celebrating the anniversary of the coronation of His Holiness.

Caravaggio and I had begun work that morning in the Palazzo Firenze when Orazio Gentileschi, a painter who was gaining some fame at the time, came over. Good-naturedly, he chided us for working on such a beautiful day. He already was pretty drunk and produced a flagon of wine. Of course, we immediately stopped work and went into the garden. Soon, the architect Onorio Longhi also arrived.

Like Caravaggio, Onorio and Orazio were notorious hot heads, reckless, and enjoyed a good party. The four of us then made our way to the playing field where we found the ever mild-mannered artist Ottavio Leoni and some other friends who were also "celebrating," which meant that they too were quite drunk and very loud.

Together, we headed down the Via della Scrofa, laughing as we passed a bottle from man to man. Some of us wanted to go to the Piazzo Navona; some wanted to go to the Campo de' Fiori. We heard that the Tomassoni gang was out and around and decided to avoid the Via di Pallacordia fearing that we would run into them. Not far from the Sant'Agostino, we heard shouting and loud cries of *"Viva il Papa; viva il Papa"* coming down the Via d'Ascanio. We could tell that it was Ranuccio, his brothers, and some of their friends. It may have been an accidental meeting, but I do not think so. I think they were looking for us and particularly for Caravaggio.

Like we, they too were drunk and began taunting and pushing us around. I swear that we tried to ignore them. They singled Caravaggio out, surrounded him, and taunted him with loud sing-song exclamations. I was surprised at his forbearance as they mocked him. Over and over, they yelled out *"Ladro! Frocio!"* Ranuccio confronted Caravaggio face to face and muttered something about the money that he was owed. He insisted on a fight and drew his sword. To call it a "duel" shows no understanding of the *rione* or its inhabitants at all. I know it was Ranuccio who started it. In response, Caravaggio drew his sword, and quickly the so-called duel became a street brawl with all of us hitting, kicking, and throwing bricks and rocks.

I saw Caravaggio's sword lunge forth to stab Ranuccio. I could see that he was aiming for the leg. Ranuccio stumbled forward, and the sword went in deeper and higher. It is not true that Caravaggio was trying to castrate Ranuccio, as has been said, but I am sure he wanted to make him lame.

To our horror blood spurted out of the wound, and Ranuccio collapsed. Chaos reigned and blood was everywhere. One Tomassoni brother, Giovan Francesco, ran to Ranuccio. He suddenly turned and attacked Caravaggio, badly wounding him in the head. Caravaggio, knife in hand, lunged toward Giovan Francesco. It took three of us to restrain him. He had murder in his eyes. I am sure that had we not held him back, Caravaggio would have killed Giovan Francesco.

Several of the brothers and their friends struggled to get Ranuccio back to the Tomassoni *palazzo*. It was obvious that Ranuccio was bleeding to death. He died very quickly.

We knew that we were in serious trouble and scattered. I do not know how, but I heard that the wounded Caravaggio managed to get to the cellar of the *palazzo* of the Marchese Giustiniani. We knew it was important to hide him, so we spread the rumor that he was in the Palazzo Madama with Del Monte.

When we heard that Ranuccio was to be buried the next day in the Pantheon, we were sure that we were in real trouble. The Pantheon was the burial place for the most influential and famous people of Rome. *Dio mio*, the great painter Raphael was buried there! Obviously Ranuccio's death was fast becoming a big deal with very highly placed people involved.

Wild rumors abounded, all exaggerated by the newspapers. The facts kept getting distorted as to who did what and to whom. More and more the criticism lay on the famous, quick-tempered, erratic painter Caravaggio. More and more Ranuccio was made out to be a fine young aristocratic man, war hero, husband, and father, who was innocently attacked.

Longhi and Gentileschi quickly left Rome. I decided to stay but to keep undercover. I thought that there would be little or no interest in me.

I did not see Caravaggio for a time, but I well knew what was happening. Everyone was talking about it, and my network of friends, especially servants in the great houses, was extensive. As I mentioned, to the "highly placed" we were invisible. They talked as though we were not there. Yet like ants, we were everywhere and took away every morsel with us. Through my "informants," I knew what was happening to Caravaggio. I also had to know if legal action were being taken against me.

Word had it that Del Monte and Giustiniani quickly had a secret meeting at the Palazzo Madama. They invited the Marchesa Colonna, who arrived hidden in a covered carriage. I heard that during the meeting, the Marchesa strongly reaffirmed that her family had long ties to the Merisi family and regarded Caravaggio as a great artist. She agreed to help. She also added that she knew of the "lawlessness" of the Tomassoni boys. She openly expressed her outrage regarding them and affirmed that she had little respect for them and their family.

The Marchesa insisted that Caravaggio go to Genoa, which was under French domination. Of course, her family was hugely influential in Genoa, and she assured Del Monte and Giustiniani that Caravaggio would be well cared for and that there would be adequate insulation from any action by the Tomassoni family. However, Del Monte worried that Caravaggio was too injured to travel such a distance, so they decided to say that he had gone to Genoa but in fact he would be hidden in the immense, fortress-like Palazzo Colonna in Zagarolo, about a day's journey southeast of Rome in the hills.

The plan was presented to Caravaggio, and he reluctantly agreed only after an exasperated Del Monte promised that Cecco could eventually join him. It was arranged that Caravaggio would escape hidden in a cart that very night. When he was loaded onto the cart, he was urged to hunch over and to cover himself with a blanket. However, to the horror of those trying to hide and protect him, Caravaggio, all bandaged up, defiantly sat bolt upright beside the driver as they raced south through the streets of Rome.

Meanwhile, Del Monte was tireless in his attempts to salvage the situation. He immediately arranged an audience with His Holiness Paul V to see if some sort of deal could be arranged. He asked Cardinal Borghese to accompany him, knowing of the cardinal's interest in art and in Caravaggio. The initial reception with the Pope was promising. The Pope listened attentively as exile was discussed. The Pope seemed to favor a commuted sentence with exile.

Shortly thereafter, the Tomassoni clan went to work. They were not to be mollified. They met with the Pope and reminded him of their long and valuable service to the papacy. They informed the Pope that not only had Caravaggio killed Ranuccio but that he had tried to kill Giovan Francesco. They reminded the Pope that Ranuccio had left a widow, the sister of a brave papist soldier, and young children. They implied that they would settle for nothing less than Caravaggio's death.

The Pope re-summoned Cardinal Borghese and Del Monte to the Vatican. They could tell that he was very annoyed by it all. He told them that he had changed his mind. One of my informants heard His Holiness say, "Caravaggio must be tried for the murder of Ranuccio!" Del Monte pleaded, "But Your Holiness, it was not intentional. It was an accidental death!" The Pope turned his back on both of them, and Cardinal Borghese moved toward his uncle and whispered something in his ear. The Pope turned suddenly and shouted, "*You* are telling *me* that it would be a great advantage to *me* and to Rome to have an extraordinary talent such as Caravaggio here! I suppose the portrait that he painted of me is your idea of an extraordinary talent!" Del Monte was aghast and tried to placate His Holiness.

Both Borghese and Del Monte continued pleading, and the Pope became increasingly furious. He blurted out, "That *frocio* caused this terrible incident to happen *and*," he stormed, "he did it on the anniversary celebration of my elevation!" Everything they said only further angered His Holiness, who repeatedly returned to his disdain for the portrait. Suddenly, with a wave of his hand, he dismissed them. As I look back on what I heard about that conversation, I think what a sorry state of affairs it was that a man's vanity was playing a critical role in the fate of a great artist.

With Caravaggio secreted away in Zagarolo, things were eerily quiet for about a month. Eventually, I felt confident enough to move around Rome rather freely. However, on 28 June 1606, the official in charge of the inquiries placed in contempt of court all those involved in the incident. Surprisingly, the Tomassoni brothers were on the list! Only Ottavio Leoni was taken to prison. With his delicate features and feminine mannerisms, the poor guy frequently was jailed because the guards knew he was good for *una scopata veloce*.

Over the next weeks, there were many rumors of plea bargaining. Everyone was astonished to learn how increasingly the Pope himself was involved. It came as no surprise when we heard that the Tomassoni sons were granted pardons, but it was a surprise to hear that Longhi and Gentileschi were also pardoned. Borghese may have had a hand in that. He was always trying to obligate any rising artistic talent.

To my horror, I also heard that the court was making inquiry about the unknown artist who was standing near Caravaggio when the fatal lunge occurred. It was widely rumored that this person would be a key witness. Having no faith in the fairness of the proceedings and knowing that it was "yours truly," I quickly made plans to leave Rome for Sicily. I was not to see Caravaggio until a year later when by chance we met in Malta.

The murder charge against Caravaggio stood, and the Tomassoni family moved in with a vengeance. Vainly, Del Monte repeatedly made pleas to the Pope attempting to make the case that the murder was not premeditated. The Tomassonis persuaded the court, really the Pope, that the absent Caravaggio be branded with the horrific sentence of *bando capitale*.

The entire artist community of Rome was stunned. How was it possible that a man who only shortly before had been heralded as the *egregius in Urbe Pictor* now was on the lam, persecuted, and subjected to a medieval fate—"That any one who recognized him and beheaded him would be rewarded." Small wonder that Caravaggio's bitterness and suspiciousness intensified. Strikingly but not surprisingly, his paintings grew darker and the theme of decapitation was to play an increasingly larger role in his work. He soon had to flee further south protected only by his talent.

Caravaggio, *Flagellation*, 1607

Chapter Six

Naples

With the authorities possibly searching for me and with the full force of the Tomassoni power and vengefulness evident everywhere, I decided it was best to return to Sicily. I was in a hurry to leave town and did not properly bid Caravaggio farewell. I wondered if I would ever see him again. Little did I know that fate would entwine us during the last months of his life.

I heard that he had headed south. I knew that he was on the lam but took heart in knowing that he was being protected by some very powerful and remarkably tolerant friends, Del Monte, Giustiniani, and the Marchesa.

The next year went well for me. On my return to Sicily, I set up a studio in Syracuse. I found a reliable if uninteresting woman, married, and soon had a small family. I developed a reputation as a technically skillful painter. The fact that I had actually worked with Caravaggio was immensely helpful in my career. Proudly, I was known as a *caravaggista*. My fame though minor spread, and I was pleased that I frequently was invited to several cities in Sicily and even to Malta to do some work.

I heard only sporadically about Caravaggio, although my informants were highly dependable and in positions to overhear important people discussing Caravaggio and his fate. It was confirmed that safe inside the Colonna estate in Zagarolo his wounds healed well under the watchful eyes of the Marchesa and her wide circle of family and acquaintances.

Although technically on the lam, almost immediately, there was no shortage of interest in his artwork. The paintings from this period tended to be small easel work, dark in texture and theme. Incredible as it seems, even under these uncertain circumstances the paintings were great.

One of them I only saw much later and is particularly close to my heart. The painting ended up in Genoa, so many think that Caravaggio went from Zagarolo to Genoa, but I do not think so. I believe that the painting arrived in Genoa because it was intended as a gift to the Doria family, relations of the Marchesa, in case Caravaggio had to flee quickly to that city.

In any case, the painting is a three-figured *Ecce Homo* in which a beautiful Jesus, beaten and crowned with thorns, is standing close to a dark-skinned attendant who is tenderly covering his shoulders with a cloth. A harsh, puzzled Pilate, painted as a northern Italian nobleman, stands to the right presenting the serene Jesus to the jeering crowd. The painting is not Caravaggio at his best; yet when I saw it, my eyes welled up with tears. I was deeply touched. I cannot help but see myself as the young attendant. I like to think that Caravaggio took me with him in his thoughts during those dark days.

Another painting completed during his stay in Zagarolo, a much better painting, is *Mary Magdalene in Ecstasy*. I first saw this painting later when Caravaggio carried it to Malta and later to Sicily. He told me the painting was Lena from memory. He did not have to. It was beautiful Lena illuminated by a harshly oblique light, her hair lightened, her slender hands clasped, and her head thrown back revealing her lovely neck. In ecstasy, her eyes are closed and her yearning lips parted. Unfortunately, I have also seen many pitiful copies of it.

To me, this painting epitomizes how tenderly Caravaggio painted women. As I have stated before, I came to recognize that under the rough, ill-tempered, arrogant, swaggering Caravaggio was a soft, fragile woman.

In Summer 1607, I heard that Del Monte and Giustiniani had decided that Caravaggio must continue south to Naples.

Naples was the largest and most commercially developing city in Italy and in the world. Its perfect harbor was filled with ships taking exports to and bringing imports from everywhere, and a strong and wealthy merchant class was developing. There was action on every level, including interest in collecting art. With the rising merchant class, there would be less concern about Council of Trent restrictions and greater appreciation for Caravaggio's novel realism. Commissions would easily be coming his way.

Of great importance was that Naples was under the Spanish viceroy, and Pope Paul V was not likely to want to interfere and upset that delicate political balance even to please the Tomassoni family. Del Monte and Giustiniani underestimated the Tomassoni clan and its influence on His Holiness in that regard.

Arriving in Naples, Caravaggio was widely welcomed. I am not sure when, but Cecco eventually joined him. Although I harbored much resentment toward Cecco, I did admire that he stuck with Caravaggio even when the future looked grim. Also by this time, I was looking at Caravaggio in a much different light. I realized that much of my attraction to him had been dependency. We were both just boys lost in the wilds of Rome clinging to each other. With time, my animosity for Cecco changed from jealousy and resentment to pity.

NAPLES

As it turned out, I heard that Cecco stayed with Caravaggio until Caravaggio left for Malta. I do not know under what circumstances they parted or what their situation was when they parted. All I know is that Cecco eventually became a minor painter known for his brutal images. Typical of him, it was not enough to present himself as a *caravaggista*. He continued to foist himself off as Cecco da Caravaggio, as though he and Caravaggio were from Caravaggio and in some way related. At this point it was a small matter, and I did not much care.

I am not sure, but I think in Naples Caravaggio stayed in a Guistiniani *palazzo* and kept a low profile. Although he forced himself to work largely without models, I am reasonably sure that Cecco posed for a *David and Goliath*. A later *David and Goliath*, painted during his second and even more problematic stay in Naples, contains a terrifying self-portrait. In that *David and Goliath*, Cecco, painted from memory, is David in deep tragic regret. It was easy to see how the sentence of *bando capitale* was affecting Caravaggio. I know of at least six decapitation paintings following sentencing.

I don't remember hearing of any quarrels or fights, and I do not think he was in jail in Naples, a real change for him; but there was a troubling story of his being commissioned by the wealthy

Croatian trader Nicolò Radolovich to paint what sounded like a very crowded Virgin and Child amidst garlands, flights of angels, and saints. If it were ever done, I do not know what happened to that painting. However, it is known that Caravaggio deposited a handsome payment from Radolovich and later was charged with illegally withdrawing funds from that account.

During this first visit to Naples, Caravaggio received an important commission for a main altar piece in the new church of the charitable co-fraternity of the Pio Monte della Misericordia. This painting is one of his most enduring masterpieces and for me has a curious autobiographic aspect.

The painting is based on Matthew's description of the six works of mercy of Jesus. The co-fraternity added from their dedication a seventh: care of the dead. The painting is the renowned *The Seven Works of Mercy*.

The large vertical painting is a complex, composite condensation of the Works. Lena's feet from *The Death of the Virgin* are easily identified as signifying "Care of the dead." I was fascinated by Caravaggio's condensing the Work of Mercy "... when I was in prison and ye came unto me" with the Work of Mercy " ... when I was hungry, you gave me food." Being in prison was a major part of Caravaggio's short life. It is to me autobiographically telling who comes to feed and comfort the prisoner. It is Pero, the epitome of Roman Charity, offering her bare breast to save her father from starvation. I guess we never give up wanting to be nursed.

I heard things seemed pretty settled during that stay in Naples, and I never heard that Radolovich took any subsequent action. For the time being, Caravaggio stayed out of trouble and was painting many commissions extremely well.

I thought the situation was quiet in Rome until I learned through informants that Cardinal Borghese let Giustiniani know very indirectly that there was some sort of a deal being made between the Pope and the Spanish Viceroy and that Caravaggio was part of the deal. Borghese was such a slippery person that it was hard to trust him. One could only count on his being on both sides of any situation.

In any case, the information was troubling enough that Giustiniani contacted Del Monte and the Marchesa Colonna for another secret meeting. Again and needless to say at their social level, there were no secrets.

In discussing where Caravaggio might go, the Marchesa emotionally reminded Del Monte and Giustiniani that her son, Fabrizio Sforza Colonna, was General of the Hospitaller galleys in Malta. We all knew the story. In some ways, it was strikingly similar to that of Caravaggio.

Fabrizio, one of Costanza's six sons, had been in trouble since childhood. As a young man, he was implicated in a number of unexplained crimes including a possible murder. In 1602, another scandal erupted, and his fate became a *cause célèbre*. The Pope wanting to get rid of the matter agreed to Fabrizio's exile to Malta. The Grand Master of the Knights of Malta, Alof de Wignacourt, was delighted with the idea of having a member of the Colonna family join his entourage. He was always happy to have rich, powerful people beholden to him.

The Marchesa related how her son prospered under the tutelage of the Knights. Seeming to mature, he quickly demonstrated administrative and leadership skills and rose to become General of the Navy for the Knights. He probably was the leader of the infamous marauding Maltese Navy, the source of slaves for slave trading that was the main commercial enterprise of the Knights.

The Marchesa indicated that she had considerable influence with the Grand Master and showed Del Monte and Giustiniani letters from him in which he wrote how delighted he was to serve her and her illustrious family. She concluded by saying that she would gladly contact her son to negotiate with Wignacourt on Caravaggio's behalf.

Things must have gone well despite, I am sure, Caravaggio's typically obstreperous questions, protestations, and ridiculous conditions. However, he also must have known that he had no options. On 12 July 1607, General Fabrizio arrived grandly in Valletta, the capital of Malta, from one of his maritime exploits with Caravaggio aboard his ship.

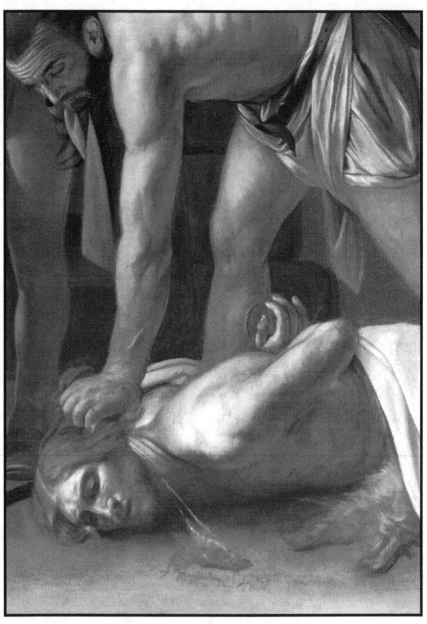

Caravaggio, *Decapitation of Saint John the Baptist* (Detail), 1608

Chapter Seven

*E*ven though Malta is close to Sicily, I really never gave it much thought until I returned to Sicily and was having some success as an artist. I learned that Malta was a rich source of commissions and was pleased that I was invited to make a couple of visits. Little did I know that Malta was to thrust Caravaggio again into the forefront of my life.

As a hopelessly bored school boy, I reluctantly learned from a nun that the Knights of Malta were established as an Italian religious order prior to the Crusades. I could not have been less interested as the poor nun droned on about them.

She enthusiastically told us that originally they were called the Knights Hospitaller and became the Sovereign Military Hospitaller Order of Saint John of Jerusalem, of Rhodes, and of Malta. With great sanctimony she told us that prior to the Crusades, the Knights went to the Holy Land to administer to wounded and ill pilgrims and gradually became prime protectors of pilgrims. She went on and on about how during the Crusades they cared for wounded and ill crusaders, emphasizing their spiritual lives. She told us that the Knights were called *fra,* that is "brother," and made them out to be near saints.

I must admit that as a boy it did intrigue me to know that from their inception, and the tradition has continued, they accepted into their ranks only sons of royal, noble, or aristocratic families from all over Europe. We all envied the noble families with their great wealth, *palazzi,* feasts, grand parties, and endless numbers of servants. Even though I knew it could never be, while the nun droned on, frequently I dreamed of being a Knight of Malta—a man of noble birth with a wonderful robe, a beautiful horse, and a member of a gallant order. Those day dreams were a life-saving refuge from the way my poor drab family lived and the constant intimidation of my always angry father. I confess that I lost interest when I was older and learned that the Knights were a monastic order pledging poverty, chastity, and obedience, and were devoted to care of the sick and dying.

Before my first visit to Malta, I checked out some of the facts about the Knights with a few friends. None of my informants had anything good to say about them. My visits to Malta quickly revealed that what the good nun thought they were and what they actually were were vastly different.

MALTA

What the nun did not tell us was that during the Crusades the Knights of Malta joined the crusaders in bloody battles to free the Holy Land from the Muslims and that by the end of the ill-fated Crusades, the Knights had become a militaristic, quasi-monastic religious order that had nothing to do. She certainly did not tell us that on returning from the Crusades, they roamed all over Europe plundering and raping as a band of high-born thugs and good-for-nothings.

My visits to Malta bore out what my informants said. Malta was a militant, multinational, noble, fraternal theocracy ruled by a grand master. As far as I could tell, few did anything.

On my visits I developed friendships with a couple of knights. One particularly friendly old knight loved to tell me about the history of the Order and the island. During one lonely long evening in a tavern, he told me after much drinking, "It was Charles V of Spain who gave the Order the island of Malta for the price of an annual single Maltese falcon."

When thoroughly drunk, sardonically he added to the tales of heroics and valor, "The King gave us Malta to rid the continent of us. He could take no more of our rampages and lawlessness." Embarrassed by what slipped out, he quickly added, "But we are extremely proud of the wars with the infidels (Muslims)." Deeply intent, he continued, "You know we survived the 1565 siege by the great Ottoman Sultan Suleiman. It was a great test of our fortitude. During the siege, most of us and the other inhabitants of the island died, but a few surviving knights held out. When victory was achieved, we moved the capital from Mdina high in the center of the island to this beautiful deep port. We built a great city here and named it Valletta after our French Grand Master Jean Parisot de la Valette, who courageously led us through those terrible times."

I knew that in recent years, restless but resigned to living on their beautiful barren island, the Knights' main vocation was plundering Arab ships plying along the north coast of Africa. They seized the cargo and hijacked the Arab crews to sell as slaves, their main vocation and source of income. I know there were about 15,000 slaves on Malta alone.

As the old knight waxed on, I thought they seemed unduly proud of the suffering that they endured. I kept silent but thought, "They use the wars with the Muslims to justify their plundering. They must be the most high-born religious pirates in history."

I came to know Valletta very well, but I never did travel to see Mdina and the magnificent cathedral that they restored. Valletta is a much more orderly place than what I was accustomed to in Sicily. The streets are long and broad and lined with beautiful stone lodges, *auberges,* in which the knights lived. Each *auberge* belongs to the nation of its origin. Most of the Knights were French or Italian and most spoke French and Italian.

The tradition of recruiting sons from European noble and aristocratic families continued, but also the Order became a refuge for sons of highly placed families who were in various kinds of trouble. General Fabrizio Sforza Colonna was an example.

During several visits to Malta, I could see that my knightly friends, although high born, were a lot like my old friends in the *rione* Campo Marzio. They were arrogant, feisty, provocative, quarrelsome young men who had nothing to do and who tended to be an unruly lot. By and large, they were useless. In fact, the entire scene in Valletta was rather like the scene in my much missed Roman *rione.* Many of the knights reminded me a lot of the Tomassoni brothers, only more friendly. As in my old *rione,* prostitution was everywhere and individual fights were common. Unlike Rome, the prostitutes largely were African young women and boys. Also unlike Rome, there was a strong, relatively uncorrupted police force so there was little or no rioting or gang fighting.

In early 1607 on a visit to Valletta seeking commissions, I confess that I got myself into a bit of trouble. I would not detail it except that my dear wife has now passed to Our Maker and the story does reveal something about Caravaggio.

As I mentioned, Valletta was a wild seaport. There were girls everywhere looking for action and money. One of them, a young African girl, seemed attracted to me. She became my temporary "wife" much to the annoyance of her brother, who insisted that I also pay for his food and lodging. It is a mystery to me how I could have gotten into this mess when I had lived that very life myself and thought I knew all the tricks. But, there I was. To make matters worse, the girl became pregnant and the brother threatened to kill me if I did not marry her. I could not tell them I was married, so we found an official and a priest and I paid both to marry us. I can tell you that the life of a bigamist, even when one's wife does not know, is not easy.

We eventually found a witch on the nearby island of Gozo who could "help." The witch was successful, but the brother learned that I had a wife in Sicily and threatened to go to the authorities charging me with bigamy. I paid him off with several paintings, but he reported me anyway. That is how I ended up before the Inquisition denying my first marriage and promising to support my African wife. All I wanted to do was to leave the whole mess behind me and return to Sicily. I had no choice but to agree to pay off both my "wife" and my "brother-in-law." Fortunately for me, they were eager for paintings.

During this time I learned that Caravaggio had been granted asylum in Malta. I thought Malta would be the perfect place for him. It was a multinational theocracy ruled by a Grand Marshal. It was a vassal state under the Spanish Viceroy of Sicily, so papal influence was indirect. It was unlikely that His Holiness would want to interfere and upset the delicate political equilibrium the Vatican had established with Spain and the Knights of Malta. Also, His Holiness certainly would not want needlessly to offend the large number of important families, like the Colonna family, who were relieved to settle their errant sons there.

In mid July 1607, Caravaggio arrived in Malta amid much celebration, as I mentioned, on the flag ship of General Fabrizio Colonna. What was amazing was that Caravaggio was personally greeted by the Grand Master Alof de Wignacourt and escorted to the Grand Master's opulent palace.

Grand Master Wignacourt, a French nobleman from Picardy, of course, was rich and powerful. He personally benefited from his fleet's raids on the Arab ships, and he eagerly collected rich gifts, actually they were bribes, from powerful Europeans who needed him to take in their unruly sons.

It was reported that Wignacourt had over 200 slaves, all

captives from ships, and over 10 pages, young boys sent to him by noble families for training and possible positions. He recently had been made Prince of the Holy Roman Empire, which earned him the title of His Serene Highness. As it turned out, His Serene Highness was also a *frocio*, a fag.

On arriving in Malta, Caravaggio was flooded with requests for paintings, largely portraits. Portraiture was a genre for which he did not much care, but it did seem that he was learning to compromise.

Fortunately, early in his stay in Malta he did a beautiful portrait of Fra Antonio Martelli, an elderly, highly placed knight. Honoring the monastic origins of the Order and being elderly and pious, Fra Martelli preferred being called *fra* rather than *cavaliere*. He was widely regarded as honorable, and although close to Wignacourt, he strongly objected to Wignacourt's accumulation of personal wealth and the means by which the Order was prospering, especially taking and selling slaves.

Eventually Fra Martelli was to welcome the opportunity to leave Malta and became a prior in Messina, where he was to prove himself an important person for Caravaggio at a time when Caravaggio needed help from important persons.

Shortly after Caravaggio arrived in Valletta, he and I

accidentally met in a tavern. He greeted me warmly. I was amazed at how prosperous he looked and how settled he seemed. However, I had known Caravaggio for a long time and knew that any semblance of stability could not last.

One evening, rather gleefully Caravaggio told me that shortly after arriving in Malta, to his surprise, he was called to appear before the Inquisition. He was relieved to learn that he was summoned there "because of *your*, let's say, marital situation." With delicious delight he emphasized the word *your*. Of course, I knew about the investigation, but I was amazed to learn that the Inquisition knew that he and I knew each other. I eagerly listened.

He told me, "They asked me if I knew you, and I told the esteemed Leonetto Corbario, the Inquisitor, whom I instantly loathed, 'No, I do not, but I know him to be an honest man.' He asked if I had seen you in Malta, and I answered, 'No, I don't associate with the likes of him.' The Inquisitor shot back, 'I thought you said he was an honest man.' I replied, 'That is why I don't associate with him and that is why I am putting up with a *stronzo* like you.' Of course, I mumbled 'putting up with a *stronzo* like you.' Corbario shot back, 'What did you say?' With feigned humility and exaggerated enunciation, I said, 'I said that is why I am pleased to be of service to a *learned doctor* like you.' The scribe practically doubled over in an attempt to stifle his laughter!"

We both laughed heartily as he continued the story. "The Inquisitor was visibly annoyed and asked, 'Is he married?' I replied, 'Of course, sir. Many times!'" Caravaggio leaned over closely to me and with an air of contempt said, "The *learned doctor* became very intent and repeated, 'Many times?' to which I replied, 'Yes, he is very pious. I know he frequently goes to church to reaffirm his marriage vows.'"

Caravaggio continued, "When the Inquisitor asked, 'Do you think he is married to a Sicilian and to an African?' I looked very serious and said, 'Is there a difference? Sicily is very close to Africa. I often can't tell a Sicilian from an African.' With that I was dismissed."

To complete the story, the court eventually dismissed my case and annulled my marriage when the extortion efforts of the brother-and-sister team became clear. I tell it because it well illustrates Caravaggio's instant rebelliousness in the face of any authority, especially arrogant authority. But mostly I tell it because I feel (hope) that it reveals that under it all, Caravaggio was always loyal to his friends. Even though I know that he could not resist taking a jab at "the learned doctor," given the circumstances, Caravaggio could have taken the easy way out and played along with the authorities to gain favor with them.

Caravaggio and I met several times while I was in Malta. In fact, I was the only friend he had in Malta. I felt he was genuinely glad to be with me and even asked me about my art and my family. He filled me in on many of the details of his leaving Rome and the flight to Naples. Mostly we talked about the art he produced since I last saw him. On one of those evenings he told me about his convalescence in Zagarolo. At that point, he showed me the wonderful *Mary Magdalene in Ecstasy* that he was carrying with him. I became teary-eyed as he told me that the painting was intended for the Marchesa Colonna. He added "You know the Magdalene is our beautiful Lena. I could not bear to part with it." It was a poignant moment for both of us, and I think I also saw tears in the eyes of the great painter.

Another night, he spoke excitedly about the *Seven Works of Mercy* he had done in Naples for the co-fraternity of the Pio Monte della Misericordia. He said, "It may be my most complex work." With a slight laugh he added, "I put Lena into it, too. If you see it, you will see that the two feet sticking out for 'Care for the dead' are Lena's feet from the *Death of the Virgin*."

Those evenings in Malta were among the most enjoyable

times I ever spent with Caravaggio, and I cherish their memory. I felt reassured that the reports from my friends about the events of his life since I last saw him were full and accurate. More so, I was glad that Caravaggio talked freely with me, something he rarely did with anyone.

However, even though Caravaggio had a sweet deal in Malta, he talked as though he were at the nadir of his life. Surprisingly, it was clear that his despondency did not affect his artistic power. As a show of appreciation to Fabrizio for making it possible for him to come to Malta, uncharacteristically Caravaggio approached Fabrizio suggesting he paint a major panel for the co-cathedral in Valletta in Fabrizio's honor. What a painting!

The Beheading of Saint John the Baptist is a large, horizontal painting with all that is best about Caravaggio. Filled with dynamic diagonals, mysterious light and revealing darkness, grieving women and contrasting ages, a nearly naked man has partially severed the Baptist's head. John's face reflects a peculiar death-induced peacefulness, as though the torment is over. From the cut throat, reverberating the terrible legal threat, *bando capitale,* streams blood running on the ground forming the letters *f michela.* In blood Caravaggio wrote, "made by Michela(ngelo Merisi)." It is as though he were admitting how much of his problems he brought on himself. Ominously, in the darkness, two prisoners—one with a bandaged head—stoically view the proceedings, wondering who will be next.

Caravaggio and I continued to meet occasionally at taverns. He told me about Wignacourt's courting him. He imitated Wignacourt's French flourishes as Wignacourt waxed on about the great future for Caravaggio in Malta and how he, Wignacourt, would make him, Caravaggio, the greatest artist in the world. Knowing of his desire to return to Rome, I was worried when Caravaggio intimated that he pledged to Wignacourt that he would remain in Malta permanently.

To everyone's surprise and to the great resentment of many of the knights, on 14 July 1608, Caravaggio was made *cavaliere di grazia* just a year after coming to Malta. The long and involved religious training, vow taking, and proofs of valor and sincerity had been put aside as Wignacourt pushed through Caravaggio's knighthood. I heard that Wignacourt personally was making strong and direct appeals for Caravaggio's pardon from the Pope. I also heard that the Tomassonis were adamant about bringing Caravaggio back to Rome for execution.

I feared that there would be problems, knowing Caravaggio's difficulty in accepting a good situation and what I heard about a rising tide of jealousy among his fellow knights. I also was concerned because I knew that Caravaggio was talking too much about one of Wignacourt's pages, a young French prince. I had seen the boy and knew he was about 14, Caravaggio's preferred age, and of fair skin and rosy cheeks. I feared Caravaggio would not be able to keep his hands off him.

In one of our meetings, Caravaggio talked about Wignacourt's posing for him half-naked as Saint Jerome. He added, "It was not hard to get him naked." I knew better than to press him about their relationship, so there was a momentary silence. He then added, "You know I like them much, much younger. Do you see the way his skin hangs? He objected mightily to my realism about that."

What did concern me was when Caravaggio told me that he had easily persuaded Wignacourt, a rather short and stocky man, to have the French page with him in his official portrait. It seemed strange that a man who was one of the most powerful people in the world would want his page in his official portrait. I intimated and Caravaggio confirmed that the boy was the Grand Master's "favorite." His tone much played on the way sultans were talked about as having a "favorite" from the harem. Caravaggio got that mischievous look in his eye that he got when he knew that he was doing something that was going to get him in trouble and wanted others to know it. I asked if he were *scopando* the boy, and he was coyly ambiguous. However, he did say, "When you see the portrait, you will see who the boy really is interested in."

When the portrait was put on display, it seemed to me a rather stiff Grand Master looking imperial in a full suit of armor. The boy is gorgeous, holding a plumed helmet with his Cross of Malta prominently displayed. The boy's red leggings add warm and vivid color to him, which is increased by the other touches of red in the painting. I thought back to Caravaggio's comment. Indeed, the handsome youth looks rather slyly not at the Grand Master but at the painter.

It was getting close to the time that I was readying myself to return to Sicily. The night before I was to leave, Caravaggio, drunk, told me that he had had a communication with Cardinal Borghese and that Borghese was working on his uncle, the Pope, to have Caravaggio pardoned so that he could return to Rome. In the bargain, Caravaggio pledged to join the Borghese household—he added ironically, as an "indentured painter."

I was frozen with fear. Why trust Cardinal Borghese? Mostly I feared how Wignacourt would respond when he found out that after all the favors and honors he was bestowing on Caravaggio and all the concessions and promises he had made to His Holiness, Caravaggio was working behind his back to return to Rome. I said little, but my expression revealed my fear. Caravaggio passed it off saying that the old fool Wignacourt would be helpless before the powerful Borghese.

I left for Sicily. Just four months later I heard that Caravaggio had been arrested for attacking a knight, Cavaliere di Giustizia. Gradually information leaked out. Giustizia had been charged by the Grand Master with discussing a delicate matter with Caravaggio and Caravaggio brutally attacked him. Caravaggio was immediately apprehended by the militia and "thrown into the dreaded *guva.*"

The *guva* is essentially a hole with a small opening at the top carved 11 feet deep into solid rock under the Fort Sant'Angelo, the fortress that is high above the harbor in the center of Valletta. The *guva* was infamous for it was a black hole used as a prison for runaway slaves, slaves who murdered their master, and errant knights who were to be executed.

On 27 November 1608, a report circulated that "Caravaggio came into conflict with a very noble knight, was placed in the *guva* for safe keeping, escaped by climbing a rope ladder, and was thought to be in Sicily."

MALTA

The report went on, "Caravaggio was tried in absentia by the Order, and a warrant was issued for his arrest. He was ordered stripped of his knight's robes and all privileges and thrown out of the Order as a foul and rotten limb." Ironically, the trial and sentencing took place in the same room where hung *The Beheading of Saint John the Baptist.*

Everyone knew that something serious had happened and that the whole story was not being told. Clearly the punishment was excessive considering the charge. There were many rumors; the most consistent was that "persons at the highest level" were involved. One of my informants told me, "It was widely known that Caravaggio was *scopando* Wignacourt's young lover."

As I read, "thought to be in Sicily," dreading the idea, I knew that I would hear from him. Indeed he did show up literally on my doorstep in Syracuse, exhausted, bedraggled, and hunted.

Caravaggio, *David with the Head of Goliath*, 1610

Chapter Eight

The Final Journey: Sicily, Naples, and Death

J knew that it was impossible for Caravaggio to have escaped the *guva* without outside help. When I asked him about it, he said, "You know how Saint Peter escaped from the prison on the Campidoglio. Well, I, too, had an angel." We were silent for a moment, and then Caravaggio uttered one word, "Fabrizio."

I became very concerned as he continued. "Fabrizio had a rope ladder dropped down into the dungeon. When I climbed out, Fabrizio whispered, 'Be very quiet. Put this on.' He handed me a monk's robe and told me to pull the hood over my head and cover my face. He said I should go to the dock where a small boat would be waiting. 'It will take you to Sicily,' he whispered."

When I heard that it was Fabrizio who arranged the escape, I was suspicious. Cautiously, I attempted to warn Caravaggio. I wondered out loud, "Why would a man who has such a favored position with the Grand Master jeopardize his future for your sake?" Angrily, Caravaggio pushed aside my suspicions, and I could tell that naively he remained deeply thankful to Fabrizio.

I settled Caravaggio into my home in Syracuse, which initially was easier than I thought. The high and powerful eagerly contacted me regarding commissions for him, and they made sure that the officials looked the other way regarding apprehending him. Always it seemed his talent would protect him.

Gradually he felt freer to roam about the city and asked to see the famous grotto of Syracuse. It was clear why he had a fascination with the grotto, a prison associated with the cruel, evil, and despotic Greek tyrant Dionysius I. He was fascinated to test the legendary acoustics of the cave.

Ancient lore maintained that the grotto had been constructed in such a way that guards at the top could listen to the whispering of the prisoners deep within. As we stood on the brim looking into the grotto and tested this acoustic phenomenon, with uncanny accuracy Caravaggio noted excitedly, "Look, the model is nature herself. To listen deep below, Dionysius made a giant human ear!" I thought what a remarkable observation. It was astonishing how easily this came to him. I could see how instantly he translated nature into an image. Such was Caravaggio's fame that immediately the grotto became known as the Ear of Dionysius.

Good fortune was rarely on Caravaggio's side, and when it was he usually destroyed it. But it was his good fortune that at the time he came to Syracuse, the Church of Santa Lucia, Syracuse's patron saint, was being restored. I had friends in the senate, and I secured the commission for Caravaggio to paint the altar piece. Without question this was a grand coup for the city. I must admit that it also greatly enhanced my reputation.

The commission was purposely vague, showing the respect that the senate had for Caravaggio's genius. He swiftly produced a masterpiece, *The Burial of Saint Lucy*. It perfectly captures the intense civic pride that Syracuse has through its association with the saint. In fact, in the city, statues of Saint Lucy are everywhere.

Lucy, martyred around 304, was buried in catacombs now under Syracuse. The story strikingly parallels that of Saint Agnes. I could not help but remember the day when we, really as boys, visited the tomb of Saint Agnes. With vividness, I remembered Caravaggio's telling me the little girl's story as his gaze turned away and his eyes filled with tears.

Like Saint Agnes, the story goes that Lucy, scarcely more than a child, was engaged to be married. In gratitude for the miraculous healing of her mother at the shrine of Saint Agatha of Catania, Lucy bestowed her large dowry on the poor. With the miraculous healing, Lucy became a Christian. Her fiancé was furious that she gave away her dowry and that she became a Christian. He ordered that she be dragged off to a brothel and threatened with rape, bestiality, and a host of horrible punishments. Nothing dissuaded Lucy from her newly found belief. Finally, she was pierced in the throat with a knife. She is a symbol of vulnerable women transcending brutality—a theme that I feel reverberates deeply in Caravaggio.

The Church of Santa Lucia was built on the site where Lucy was martyred. In the reconstruction of the church, Caravaggio's painting for the altar perfectly captures the theme that is specifically cherished by the people of Syracuse.

Four hundred years after her martyrdom, Lucy's miraculously preserved body was discovered and eventually taken to Venice, where a magnificent church was erected and a rival cult developed. What is remarkable is that the painting is a dramatic portrayal of the original burial of Saint Lucy in Syracuse. It is, of course, the original burial in our city that is the part of the story dearest to the hearts of Syracusians.

Even though the painting brought Caravaggio great acclaim,

THE FINAL JOURNEY: SICILY, NAPLES, AND DEATH

I noticed that he was getting restless and impatient. He constantly hounded me and my poor wife as he kept looking for a word or any indication from Cardinal Borghese that his pardon was in process or at least being considered. Having no trust in Borghese, I was more and more uneasy that there would be no pardon. I attempted to make inquiries through my contacts in Rome and Sicily, but to little avail.

I tried to discuss the matter with Caravaggio, but I knew that any attempt to question Borghese's reliability would only infuriate him. What alarmed me more was that increasingly Caravaggio intimated that I was keeping messages from him. Several times he stormed out of the house shouting: "You would be nothing if I were to leave! You would be known as nothing but a second-rate *caravaggista*! You keep me here because of the advantage you get from being associated with me!" His words hurt me deeply and terrified my poor wife. More so, they worried me because I knew how easily Caravaggio's suspiciousness could become malignant.

My concern grew, and the great painter's irritation with me increased. I decided to travel to Messina to talk with Fra Martelli. I found the Knights' priory at Saint Mary of the Germans. I knew of the long and complex association between Sicily and the Knights. In fact, Malta and Gozo had been a part of the Kingdom of Sicily when they were given to the Knights; yet, strangely the Order possessed little property in Sicily and the present political ties were fragile. Even knowing this, however, I was surprised at how run down the priory was.

The elderly and gentle Fra Martelli received me cordially in his private rooms. Even though I knew that in Malta, of all the influential knights, Martelli lived most closely to Augustinian rules, I was surprised at how obviously spartan were his rooms. Even as the Grand Prior of Messina, his monasticism prevailed.

Fortunately for Caravaggio, Martelli was long an admirer. He treasured and kept with him the portrait Caravaggio had painted of him early in his stay in Malta. Without hesitation, Martelli welcomed the idea that Caravaggio come to Messina under his protection. Fra Martelli would soon regret his invitation, although the timing was none too soon for my own household.

Strong contentions existed between my dear wife and Caravaggio from the beginning of his arrival in Sicily. Although the soul of patience, she found it hard to tolerate the painter's slovenliness, rudeness, and arrogance. Always she waited until I was home and we were alone to complain about him.

One day on my return, she met me at the door weeping, and it was with apprehension that I heard that she and Caravaggio had fought bitterly over nothing. I must admit that it came as a great relief when she told me that Caravaggio had packed up his few belongings, cursed her and our family, and stormed out of the house muttering, "I am on my way to Messina." Apparently, he counted on Martelli's receiving him.

Nevertheless, my thoughts of personal relief alternated with genuine concern about my friend. For Caravaggio, things could only go from bad to worse.

Shortly after his arrival in Messina, I heard Martelli was contacted by a very rich merchant from Genoa, Giovanni Battista de' Lazzari, asking if Caravaggio would consider a commission for the high altar chapel in the church of Padri Crociferi, ironically a Hospitaller's church. Either word had not yet spread about Caravaggio's expulsion from the Order, or more likely, the events in Malta were being ignored because of the prospect of getting a painting.

Lazzari requested a Madonna and Saint John, his namesake. Caravaggio insisted that the commission play on the Lazzari name and not on Lazzari's namesake Giovanni Battista. He told Lazzari that he could do a "magnificent" *The Resurrection of Lazarus*. Lazzari was intimidated by the greatness of Caravaggio's reputation and readily agreed. Enthusiastically and fortunately for art, he gave

~143~

Caravaggio "free rein." The excitement about his doing the painting was experienced all over Sicily. It was no surprise that Caravaggio was provided an excellent room and studio in the church. Everywhere he was treated like a celebrity.

However, the commission did not go smoothly. There were ugly rumors that Caravaggio forced the models to hold a cadaver that had been dead four days because the Gospel of John reports Lazarus "was four days dead." There were accusations that even though the models were ill from the stench of the decaying body, Caravaggio forged ahead ignoring their fainting and retching. It was also rumored that when a group of artists came to see the painting and made minor criticisms, he, enraged, slashed it with a knife. It was also said that in three days (like Christ's resurrection) without models he painted a completely new painting. Having posed for Caravaggio and having spent months in studios with him and knowing how deranged he could become, I sadly had to agree that the rumors probably were true.

Later when I saw the painting, I knew that it was a masterpiece. The painting is crowded with figures separated and delineated by light. A young man supports the diagonal body of the young Lazarus. In response to Jesus's commanding finger, Lazarus's right arm is up-raised. Life is re-entering his body. Yet, his left arm hangs limply in death! Although there is perfection in the modeling of Lazarus's body, it is a body coming back from death. Always the master of realism, Caravaggio never feared painting death. The tenderness portrayed as Mary Magdalene touches her face to the face of her dead brother is ineffable.

I recalled the early painting, *The Calling of Matthew*, in which I am the young boy. In *The Resurrection of Lazarus*, as in *The Calling*, the figure of Jesus is minimized. It is the act that is compelling. Again, I saw the outstretched finger of Jesus as Caravaggio's brush bringing forth miracles. With great sadness, I thought of what had happened to Caravaggio—a rising star, now transformed into a hunted, haunted genius without a home.

Hearing more and more about how deranged Caravaggio had become, I went to Messina in search of him. I met with Martelli who could only express deep concern. When I returned to Syracuse, with great alarm I heard that Caravaggio had been caught by a "mob" in Messina and badly beaten. It was obvious that he would have been killed had the police not been called by some passer-by. The idea that the attack was a random event did not sit right with me. Why would a mob attack a painter? I was sure that Caravaggio was being pursued.

Not too long after, I received a letter from Fra Martelli

reflecting great worry about Caravaggio's mental state. Martelli wrote that Caravaggio talked incessantly about going to Rome. With alarm the letter continued, "Caravaggio is sure that Borghese has secured the pardon from the Pope." He added, "I must swear you to secrecy for both of our sake. I am sure I saw Giustizia and two of Fabrizio's henchmen, Fra Joannes Honoret and Fra Blasius Suarez, on the street. They quickly ducked away, not wanting to be recognized. I know that at the trial Honoret and Suarez were charged with Caravaggio's recapture. I fear Giustizia is under orders to kill Caravaggio." I felt sure that the "mob" attack was the Knights.

Somehow in all of this, Caravaggio produced *The Adoration of the Shepherds* for the high altar of the Capuchin monastery of Santa Maria La Concezione. Reflecting the vows of an order known for austerity, the birthplace is bleak and desolate. Yet as always, there is a sweet tenderness in Caravaggio's Virgin, who appears small and frail with faint halo, holding the swaddled infant. The infant looks into the mother's face most yearningly. Beside a weary Joseph are a few peasant onlookers and a donkey and an ox. The scene is the cold of mid-winter; the light faint, but spiritual. It seemed impossible that even under the greatest duress, burdened by the most outlandish circumstance, many of his making, Caravaggio's art continued to flourish.

On viewing *The Adoration*, I could not help thinking about Polidoro da Caravaggio, another great painter from Caravaggio whose life was riddled with tragedy. The grouping of the shepherds in Polidoro's great nativity, *The Persepe*, in the Santa Maria dell'Altobasso in Messina, painted some seventy years ago seems closely related to the grouping of Caravaggio's shepherds in the painting for the Capuchins.

Polidoro, a laborer who became a gifted student of the great Raphael, fled Rome when it was sacked in 1527 by Charles V. He landed in Naples and then moved on to Messina where he painted a great Crucifixion. Giorgio Vasari reported that Polidoro worked and saved money to return to Rome. The story in Messina is that he was robbed by an assistant, Tonno Calabrese, and murdered in his bed in Messina. There is no point to the story other than the eerie sense of parallel impending doom surrounding Caravaggio. I cannot help but think that Polidoro was on Caravaggio's mind during that terrible time.

In Messina, I heard matters quickly grew worse. Martelli sent me a report that was being circulated. It described an episode between a grammar school teacher, Don Carlo Pepe, and Caravaggio. Don Pepe was attending some boys playing in a field.

He noticed that Caravaggio was overly interested in watching the boys. Don Pepe approached Caravaggio, and Caravaggio said that he was studying their play for a painting. Don Pepe accused Caravaggio of stalking the boys. Caravaggio became furious and assaulted Don Pepe. The police were called, and Caravaggio was detained and a report filed. After a lengthy interrogation, he was released to Martelli. Shortly thereafter, I received a frantic message from Fra Martelli. It contained only a simple sentence and no signature, "I am at wits' end."

Adding greatly to despair, I heard that Caravaggio had accused Martelli of taking advantage of him. He charged that the elderly knight was keeping Cardinal Borghese's messages from reaching him. He accused Martelli of keeping him in Messina because of the "great prestige you receive by my presence here." In a rage, Caravaggio left the Saint Mary of the Germans priory and fled to Palermo.

It all sounded too familiar and bode catastrophe. It meant that now Caravaggio was without Martelli's or any highly placed person's protection. I am not sure how long he was in Palermo or with whom, but it was long enough to paint a rather unimpressive and overly Mannerist *Nativity with Saint Francis and Saint Lawrence.*

At this point, I had lost all contact with Caravaggio. I heard no more other than that paintings were being created and sold; however, I was skeptical. I know that many were painting in his style and foisting them off as his.

After several months, word came to me that Caravaggio had returned to Naples in late Summer 1609. I had no information as to how he got there, but I feared it was what I now considered the delusional pursuit of the pardon from Borghese. Fortunately for him, the Marchesa Colonna happened to be visiting in Naples. Again, she came to his rescue.

It was said that he was welcomed at the Colonna Palazzo Cellammare at Chiaia north of Naples and that he was actively painting. More ominously, I also heard that he wandered the streets, a frightened, pitiful figure stopping even complete strangers and asking them if Borghese had sent them to find him. Yet without question, Caravaggio produced some remarkable paintings in the next eight months.

An artist friend told me that the Count of Benevente, the viceroy of Spain in Naples, was restoring the crypt of Saint Andrew in Amalfi. Everyone acclaimed it when the count commissioned Caravaggio to paint a large *Crucifixion of Saint Andrew* for the crypt even though everyone also knew of his sorry mental condition.

I was able to see the painting a few years later. What a

magnificent piece. Andrew's face is filled with exhaustion and despair. The onlookers, including a nobleman, are astonished. They are still reeling from the powerful last words of the saint bound to the Latin cross.

There was also a dark *The Martyrdom of Saint Ursula.* I never saw this piece, but I heard that it contained a self-portrait. I was told that Caravaggio is the guard peering over the saint's shoulder trying to see her death-delivering wound. It is as though Caravaggio were asking, "How will I die?"

Word had it that there were also two horrifying decapitation paintings, a *Salome* and a *David and Goliath.* I also heard that there was a third, a *Herodias Decapitating Saint John,* but I know little of it. There is small doubt that Caravaggio in those final days was obsessed with death and decapitation.

Later to my horror, I read a newspaper report that late one night outside the famous Taverna del Cerriglio on the Vicolo di Santa Maria la Nova in Naples, Caravaggio was "assailed by a gang of hoodlums and knifed to death." The date given was 24 October 1609. I was grief stricken. When I heard the words "gang of hoodlums," I thought back on the "mob" in Messina and became very suspicious.

Clearly someone wanted Caravaggio dead, but who and

why? I now fully joined Martelli in thinking that it was the work of the Order. Who else would be so incredibly persistent as to attack him several times in Sicily and then follow his every move in Naples?

A few days later a report circulated that "the initial report of Caravaggio's death was exaggerated." The new report stated that "Caravaggio had been attacked and badly disfigured by knife wounds to the face." The report mentioned that "seriously wounded, he managed to get back to the Palazzo Cellammare and was recovering."

I heard no further news until August when I learned that Caravaggio died on 18 July 1610.

Following his death there was a flood of rumors. Various newspapers ran accounts, all contradictory and filled with inconsistencies. Angrily, I followed them carefully. I was stunned when the "official account" was issued. Nowhere did it say who issued the report.

It read: "Caravaggio went to Malta, where he was invited to pay his respects to the Grand Master and to make his portrait. Whereupon this prince, as a sign of gratitude, presented him with the Mantle of Saint John and made him a *cavaliere di grazia.*

"Here, following some sort of disagreement with the

Cavaliere di Giustizia, Michelangelo was put into prison. He managed to escape at night by means of a rope ladder and fled to the island of Sicily.

"In Palermo he painted some works. But since his enemies were chasing him, he decided to return to Naples. There they finally caught up to him, wounding him on the face with such severe slashing that he was almost unrecognizable.

"Despairing of revenge for this vindictive act and with all the agony he had experienced, Caravaggio packed his few belongings and boarded a little boat in order to go to Rome where the Cardinal Fernando Gonzaga was negotiating with His Holiness Pope Paul V for his pardon.

"On the beach where he arrived, he was mistakenly captured and held for two days in prison. When he was released, his boat was no longer to be found. This made him furious, and in desperation he started out along the beach under the fierce heat of the July sun, trying to catch sight of the vessel that carried his belongings. Finally, he came to a place where he was put to bed with a raging fever, and so without the aid of God or man, in a few days, he died, as miserably as he had lived."

I was outraged. The "official report" and the subsequent articles published were filled with obvious omissions, ambiguities, and inconsistencies. I made numerous inquires before I was able to learn that it was believed that Caravaggio had died in Palo, north of Rome. I tried to make contact with the authorities in Palo. I thought the least I could do for my old friend, to whom I was much indebted, was to take his remains to Caravaggio for burial beside his father, grandfather, and mother.

The officials in Palo did not respond to my requests for information. The same was true of inquiries at Port'Ercole.

I contacted Fra Martelli, and he also did not respond. I could not afford to travel myself, but I called upon friends in Rome. One of my old hustler friends, a man who knew the ways of the police and officials, offered to investigate. He had a friend who had a friend. The network of the underworld in Italy can be vastly more efficient than any official inquiry. He wrote that in neither Palo nor Port'Ercole was there information about the boat, Caravaggio's arrest, or his death. Repeatedly, he was told that there was no information about what happened to the body. Obviously all records, if any had been made at all, had been removed and probably destroyed.

Caravaggio, *Portrait of Alof de Wignacourt,*
Grand Master of the Order of Malta, with His Page, c. 1608

Chapter Nine

The Man Who Killed Caravaggio

J was stunned and forlorn. I knew that something terrible had happened. I was convinced that a massive cover-up was in process, and I had no one with whom I could talk.

It seemed obvious that the stories of the false arrest and the fever were trumped up. Glaringly omitted in the reports were the three attempts on Caravaggio's life that I knew about. All that was mentioned was "since his enemies were chasing him, he decided to return to Naples." Who were these enemies in Sicily? Who were the thugs who attacked him in Naples? Was it not obvious that they would be the same "enemies"? Was it not obvious that he was being pursued? What did they mean by false arrest? How could there be no record of it? What did they mean that he died in a "place"? How could they not know where he died? Where was the body? How could the body of the most famous painter in Italy mysteriously disappear?

In desperation, I decided to contact Fra Martelli in Messina. Being highly placed in the Order and an intimate of the Grand Master, I thought he might have more recent or at least more accurate information. It was difficult travel. When I arrived in Messina, before seeing him I wanted once again to visit *The Resurrection of Lazarus* in the Padri Crociferi church. Seeing it brought back many poignant memories. As always, I was deeply moved by Jesus's pointing finger. I thought of those heady days in the Palazzo Madama and the excitement we all experienced when Caravaggio received the commission for the San Luigi dei Francesi. As I looked at Christ, as in *The Calling of Matthew*, again Caravaggio was saying to me, "Follow me." This time it was as though he were saying "Don't desert me." I felt re-dedicated to finding out what had happened to my friend Caravaggio.

Again, Martelli graciously invited me into his private quarters. We had a sad meeting. He seemed depressed and weary. He talked endlessly about his advancing age and how he longed to retire soon to his family estates near Florence.

Rather suddenly, he leaned over and softly said, "I know something about Caravaggio's fate. You must swear to God that you will tell no one!" His voice and hands trembled as he with great seriousness continued in almost a whisper, "Both of our lives would be in grave danger if it were known that I had told you." An interminable silence followed.

Slowly he continued, "Before I left Malta for this position, I had an audience with Grand Master Wignacourt. I was asked to wait in an anteroom, but I could hear him shouting to Fabrizio. I could tell that the Grand Master was livid, using Italian I had never heard from him before. He was yelling, 'That *puttano* had given me his pledge that he would stay in Malta. He agreed that together we would build a great art center here. I made all kinds of compromises and promises and gave him every advantage.' I knew they were talking about Caravaggio.

"I heard Wignacourt shout, 'I made all kinds of concessions to His Holiness to get a pardon for him. His Holiness kept stalling, demanding one thing after the other. And then I learned that all the time that *frocio* was contacting that *merda* Borghese saying that he wanted to come to Rome. Borghese had extracted a pledge from him that he would work solely in Borghese's household.'

"Hardly controlling his rage, Wignacourt blurted out, 'I want him dead and I want him dead now.'

"Fabrizio replied calmly in that monotonous tone of his, 'That is a very bad idea. It would put a stain on you, the Knights, and on Malta that would never wash off.'"

Martelli continued, "Fabrizio lowered his voice, but I could make out most of what he said. He suggested that Caravaggio be imprisoned and that he, Fabrizio, arrange an escape to Sicily. Giustizia would gladly undertake the job of killing Caravaggio in Sicily where he could easily find Sicilian thugs who wanted to collect the bounty money that hung over Caravaggio's head. It would look like a gang affair and it would be on foreign soil."

I was dumbstruck as I realized that what Fra Martelli was telling me explained much. Caravaggio had told me that it was Fabrizio who arranged his escape and who but Fabrizio was in a position to arrange the boat to Sicily. Sad, angry, and powerless to do anything, I left the old man with my promise to keep the secret.

As I left, I turned and asked, "I heard that there were several paintings on the boat. I heard that Caravaggio was taking them to Borghese as a present. What do you know about them?"

Martelli looked away. After a pause his answer was a short, "I know nothing!" I suspected that he was hiding what he knew.

I knew from a friend, a Neapolitan painter, that he had heard from friends that Caravaggio had carried important paintings with him onto the boat. He had told me that Caravaggio told anyone who would listen that he was taking *Mary Magdalene in*

THE MAN WHO KILLED CARAVAGGIO

Ecstasy to Rome as a thank-you present for Cardinal Borghese for obtaining his long-sought-after papal pardon. Also I heard from friends that a *David with the Head of Goliath* was said to be on the boat. Later I saw this horrific, clearly autobiographical, painting. The painting vividly remained in my mind. In it, a sad and forlorn Cecco, painted from memory, holds Caravaggio's severed head, eyes still open and mouth gaping. The painting is both frightening and poignant. When I saw it, I almost wept to realize how precious Cecco had been to Caravaggio. Rather than a stranger being his executioner, he is killed by someone he loved. It is bizarre, but also ineffably tender. I thought "Cecco is there beside him to the very end." Only someone who actually knew Caravaggio could understand his kind of "love." Cecco is the executioner, and in a macabre way he is with him at the very end.

Some said that on the boat were two paintings of a young *John the Baptist,* easily identified as Cecco, and an incredibly painful *Salome with the Head of Saint John the Baptist,* all of which were painted during those terrible last days in Naples. I never saw the *Salome* painting, but I was told that on a golden salver is again an autobiographical Saint John's head. A painter friend who saw it in Naples said that he knew Lena somewhat modified was Salome. Like Cecco, Lena was painted from memory. I could not help but think that as in the final *David with the Head of Goliath,* Caravaggio was telling us that he would rather be killed by someone he loved than by a stranger or enemy. Like Cecco, Caravaggio placed Lena close to him at his very death. Little did he know that she died in Rome in the home of her sister on Via dei Greci in 1610, just before Caravaggio was murdered.

Everywhere I looked there was more and more of a stone wall surrounding any information. I tried to check and learned that the record of Caravaggio's trial in Malta had mysteriously disappeared from the Order's carefully guarded archives.

Over time and with repetition, despite its incredulity, the "running on the beach" and "fever" story became the official story of his death. Yet, much talk and many rumors continued regarding Caravaggio's death and the fate of the paintings. I could not rest easy, but I knew there was little I could do.

The only moment that seemed to offer hope of revealing the true story came with publication of a puzzling note from the church and monastery of Santi Apostoli in Naples. In the note, the fathers claimed that Caravaggio "had received 100 *scudi* to do a painting for them but because he was *murdered* (my emphasis) the church lost the money and the picture." I did not know what to make of it. Nothing came of it, but it was some relief to know that at least

THE MAN WHO KILLED CARAVAGGIO

someone beside me suspected murder.

With great excitement, one day I heard that the artworks said to be aboard the boat had suddenly and mysteriously appeared. As to be expected, there was much talk and squabbling over the paintings. To my astonishment, I learned that they were under the custody of Fra Vincenzo Carafa, the Knight Prior of Capua, a major priory of the Knights. To me, this was clear evidence that after the Knights murdered Caravaggio, they took the paintings to their stronghold in Capua! I thought back on my visit with Fra Martelli and his saying that he knew nothing about the fate of the paintings. I now thought he must have known about Carafa and the paintings and he lied to me to protect the Order.

Fra Carafa openly and audaciously tried to keep the paintings. He claimed that because Caravaggio was a *cavaliere di grazia*, the Order had a right to the paintings. Fortunately, the Marchesa Colonna courageously spoke out. She reminded the Knights that they had humiliated, defrocked, imprisoned, and expelled Caravaggio from the Order. I believe that she was able to get the *Mary Magdalene in Ecstasy* that had been painted for her at her family estate in Zagarolo. If anyone deserved paintings, it were she.

The fate of the two decapitation paintings, *David with the*

Head of Goliath and *Salome with the Head of Saint John the Baptist,* is more interesting. Many had heard that in his ranting in Naples, Caravaggio had said that he was going to send the autobiographical *David with the Head of Goliath* to the Grand Master. The Knights eagerly spread the story that Caravaggio wanted to make amends with the Grand Master. They concocted an elaborate story. Imagine, they had the nerve to suggest that the paintings were Caravaggio's attempt to gain forgiveness for the trouble he caused and to repay the Grand Master for all the kindnesses and honors that he had bestowed upon Caravaggio.

I knew that was the Order's feeble attempt to erase any trace of culpability. I said that if it were a gift to the Grand Master, anyone who knew Caravaggio would have known that it was his way of saying, "If you want my head, here it is!"

As one would expect, Cardinal Borghese made off like a bandit, literally and figuratively. I heard that he claimed one of the *Saint John the Baptist* paintings and "bought" the *David with the Head of Goliath.* Borghese said that he was owed the paintings because of his hard work on obtaining the papal pardon for Caravaggio. He spoke at length about his pleadings with his uncle, the Pope, always reminding the Pope what an "artistic treasure" Caravaggio's presence in Rome would be.

THE MAN WHO KILLED CARAVAGGIO

I wish I could have seen the face of the Grand Master when he heard about Borghese's bewailing Caravaggio's death as a great loss to Rome, never mentioning that Malta had given him asylum when he had to escape Rome. Also, I can tell you that the Tomassoni clan did not take kindly to the idea that the death of Caravaggio was any kind of a "loss." Incidentally, no evidence of any pardon was ever produced!

I am not sure about the fate of *Salome with the Head of Saint John the Baptist*, but the other *Saint John the Baptist* was reported to have been claimed by the Count of Lemos, the viceroy of Naples, renown as the patron of the great Spanish writer Miguel de Cervantes. I imagine it will not long be in Italy.

I also heard that in order to placate other claimants, the Count ordered Baldassare Aloisi, better known as Galanino, to make several copies of *David with the Head of Goliath* and the *Saint John the Baptist* in his possession. I can hardly imagine the problems that all these copies are going to cause in the future.

My sad story of Caravaggio's tragic life ends strangely. In 1630, some twenty years after Caravaggio's death and eight years after Wignacourt's death, I received a letter from Fra Martelli in Florence. It included specific instructions that the letter must be destroyed immediately after reading it, which I did not. It read as follows:

> To a loyal friend of the great painter Caravaggio:
>
> I am near death and have a terrible burden of conscious that I must unload. I want someone to know the truth about the end of Caravaggio.
>
> When you and I visited in Messina shortly after Caravaggio's death, I told you some of the facts about Caravaggio's last days. It is with great guilt that I tell you now that I knew more than I let you know at that time. As I face Our Maker, I swear that I was not a direct party to Caravaggio's death. In fact, try as I might, I was not successful in obviating it. I only wish I could have done more.
>
> In that Grand Master Wignacourt has passed to Our Maker and the Order has changed a good deal, perhaps the full truth regarding the death of your friend can safely be known. I knew that the French prince was Wignacourt's boy-lover, and I knew that Caravaggio seduced him. The boy came to me for confession frantic with fear for his life. He told me that Wignacourt could hardly stand to have been cuckolded by Caravaggio and furiously attacked the boy and swore to kill Caravaggio. I advised the young prince quickly to return to France, which he did. Of course, I told no one about our meeting.
>
> In Messina, it was a lie when I told you that I was in an anteroom and overheard the plotting of Wignacourt and Fabrizio regarding Caravaggio. In fact, I was directly involved in discussing what to do about

THE MAN WHO KILLED CARAVAGGIO

the "Caravaggio matter."

I told you that Wignacourt was rageful when he learned that Caravaggio was communicating with Borghese about arranging a pardon so that he could return to Rome. However, in Messina I said that I overheard Wignacourt ranting to Fabrizio. In fact, I was in the room with Wignacourt and Fabrizio.

Wignacourt was adamant that Caravaggio needed to die, and the sooner the better. Fabrizio eagerly agreed. I repeatedly pleaded for leniency, but Wignacourt would not hear of it. His ears were only for Fabrizio, who clearly was trying to gain favor with the Grand Master.

I told you Fabrizio suggested the idea of his arranging the escape from Malta and getting Caravaggio to Sicily. That was not the case. When I saw that my pleading was futile, I suggested that Fabrizio help Caravaggio escape to Sicily. I told the Grand Master and Fabrizio that I knew that Borghese was doing nothing for Caravaggio. To calm the Grand Master, I insinuated that Caravaggio would be treated as a criminal in Sicily. I suggested that it was likely that Caravaggio would be killed on the street by a gang looking for the bounty of the bando capitale *judgment that haunted Caravaggio. I also reminded the Grand Master that the Tomassoni clan was looking for Caravaggio. I said that I was sure the "Caravaggio matter" would thus be solved one way or the other and the Order and Malta, meaning Wignacourt, would be free of stain.*

THE MAN WHO KILLED CARAVAGGIO

Fabrizio and Wignacourt quickly agreed with the plan. Their manner led me to believe that they had something more sinister in mind, but I knew that I must keep quiet. At that point, Wignacourt turned to me. With a deeply penetrating look he reminded me of my vow of obedience and swore me to secrecy about the meeting. I knew that the Grand Master was insinuating that he would have me killed if I did not keep silent. Without another word, Wignacourt dismissed me. I suspected then that the two men were plotting to assassinate Caravaggio in Sicily.

I am sure you remember that I told you I saw Giustizia, Honoret, and Suarez in Messina and that they ducked away so as not to be recognized. That confirmed my suspicion that Wignacourt was out to kill Caravaggio, but I was helpless.

As it turned out, Wignacourt and Fabrizio grossly underestimated the reception that Caravaggio received in Sicily. As we well know, Caravaggio immediately had powerful protection because of the desire of many important people for his paintings. I take heart's comfort from the fact that I, like yourself, for no motive other than out of compassion, was one of the several who gave him safe haven and tried to protect him.

I knew that little, really nothing, was being done by Borghese toward the pardon. When Caravaggio came to me in Messina, I tried to warn him that Borghese was not helping him and could not be trusted. He would not listen. In fact, at one point he violently accused me of trying to *undermine his chances of returning to Rome and to keep him in Sicily to enhance my prestige.*

Because of his fame and street smarts, not to mention that Caravaggio was a furious fighter, Giustizia's murderous attempts in Messina repeatedly failed. You know of three, and I know there were more. I know that Wignacourt's impatience with Giustizia was increasing. Without question, Caravaggio's mental state deteriorated precariously following the incident with Don Carlo Pepe and the boys at the school. He became a profound embarrassment to me, and I found that I was powerless to protect him any longer. Further, I could not reason with him.

Impulsively and without informing me, he went to Palermo where he painted for a short time. I really do not know how or where he lived but assume that again patrons eager for paintings took him in and protected him. I do know that he was fixated on the idea that Borghese's representatives were waiting for him in Naples to take him to Rome for the pardon, which I knew was delusion. If Borghese were making attempts with His Holiness, they were, indeed, feeble. I heard that he enlisted the aid of young Cardinal Fernando Gonzaga in this matter, but I am not sure of that. Borghese was not one to do much for anyone but himself. Certainly he would never have done anything that might jeopardize his relationship with his uncle, the Pope.

How Caravaggio actually got to Naples I cannot imagine, but there he wandered the streets wildly claiming that Borghese had a pardon for him. In his ranting, he boasted that all he had to do was to get to Rome. In Naples, Giustizia's murderous thugs struck again, and as you know this time nearly succeeded. I am sure you remember the report that Caravaggio had been killed on leaving a Neapolitan tavern.

Fortunately for Caravaggio, the Marchesa Colonna was visiting in Naples at the time, and the severely wounded Caravaggio was taken in at the Palazzo Colonna. Nevertheless, his mental state steadily deteriorated and he often ran wildly in the streets, begging anyone he met to take him to Rome for his pardon. Meanwhile, Giustizia felt pressured by and increasingly feared Wignacourt's wrath for the failed assassination attempts. He knew how intolerant the Grand Master was of subordinates who did not carry out his orders. For Wignacourt, no reason was acceptable when his bidding was not done.

Dismayed by Caravaggio's continuing ability to fight off attacks from thugs even with his serious physical wounds and deteriorated mental state, Giustizia realized that he had to be more cunning. Using Caravaggio's fixed idea that a pardon awaited him in Rome, Giustizia saw the perfect opportunity.

Vulnerable and crazed, Caravaggio was approached by Giustizia's men in disguise. Taking advantage of his delusional state, they deceived him into thinking that they were sent by Borghese and that they would

THE MAN WHO KILLED CARAVAGGIO

take him to Rome for the pardon. They told Caravaggio that the Cardinal had arranged for a small boat to take him and his precious "gifts" to Rome. I think I can see Fabrizio's hand in creating such a clever scheme.

The rest was easy. On the way north Caravaggio was told that the boat had to stop at Palo, a remote and deserted marshy port north of Rome. He was told that the Borghese people would be waiting there with his pardon. When Caravaggio went ashore, Giustizia's henchmen ambushed and killed him. My guess is that they loaded the body back into the boat, sewed it into a leather bag, and dumped it at sea—the traditional way that the Knights treat traitors to their cause. Who knows? All I know is that the body disappeared.

After the dastardly deed was done, they put into Port'Ercole. There, they fabricated the story of the false arrest, his running on the beach, and his catching and dying of a fever.

Caravaggio's many enemies and ever-envious friends were glad to be rid of him and helped spread the story of an ignominious end to his life. His supporters thinking that it was best not to stir up trouble, or like me fearful for their lives, joined in a conspiracy of silence. I am not sure, but I suspect that Borghese in exchange for silence received the painting David with the Head of Goliath. *To justify his receiving the painting, Borghese made sure that the story was widely circulated about how he was working behind the scenes through the young Cardinal Fernando Gonzaga and had obtained the pardon—a pardon never seen by anyone.*

I came to learn the details of Caravaggio's last days through an uncanny coincidence. Fra Francesco dell'Antella, a highly placed knight and Florentine secretary to Wignacourt and a friend of Carafa, befriended Caravaggio in 1608 when Caravaggio first came to Malta. Dell'Antella, of course, was interested in a painting.

The two spent many hours together drinking and criticizing the behavior of the Knights. They talked sarcastically about the hypocrisy of the Knights. They joked about how the Knights daily violated their vow of celibacy saying that they loro avrebbero scopato *anything that walked.*

At a point, Dell'Antella asked for a painting and Caravaggio painted for him a strange Sleeping Cupid. *Actually, the Cupid is in a sleep of death. Cupid lies next to his bow with a broken string. The painting was meant to show how the Knights' behavior killed romantic love. It is a wonderful although eerie painting, and Dell'Antella rightly prized it highly.*

In July 1611, about a year after Caravaggio's death and as I am about to depart Messina for Florence, to my astonishment Dell'Antella showed up at my home. He was a terrified man, filled with fears that he was being pursued by the Knights. In desperation, he came to me because he had heard that I had given Caravaggio safe haven. Panicked, he said, "I know what happened to Caravaggio and fear the same for me!"

He then told me that one week ago, while sleeping, he was attacked by Fra Henri Lancry de Bains, a nephew of Wignacourt, over a trivial disagreement. I knew Henri, and I knew many were afraid of him because of his hot temper.

Dell'Antella tearfully confessed, "In self-defense, I killed Henri. Immediately Wignacourt came to my defense and arranged for me to leave Malta and get to Sicily. Yesterday, a gang of French-speaking hoods attacked me, and I narrowly escaped with my life. I am sure Wignacourt, while seeming to protect me, secretly planned to have me killed. It is like what he did to Caravaggio when he arranged for Fabrizio to get him out of Malta and to his death."

I asked him, "What do you mean 'what he did to Caravaggio'?"

In detail, he related how after many failed assassination attempts in Sicily and the failed assassination attempt in Naples, Giustizia's men deceived Caravaggio into thinking that they were sent there by Borghese and that there was a boat waiting to take him to Rome for his pardon. In fact, he was being taken to Palo and to his death.

Knowing from the inside the way Wignacourt worked, I gained confidence in what Dell'Antella was saying. What he told me about Caravaggio's death confirmed my suspicions.

Sensing his desperation, I promised to help Dell'Antella and *arranged his return to Florence, where I had considerable influence. I*

suggested that the painting, Sleeping Cupid, *might help him in dealing*

with the De Medici. Eventually, I was able to arrange a position in

Florence for Dell'Antella at the Accademia del Disegno for which he was

suitably grateful.

> *Minniti, you now have all the facts about what happened to your*
> *friend. In short, Grand Master Alof de Wignacourt had Caravaggio*
> *murdered! Now, it is with a heavy, but less-burdened heart that I close*
> *this letter.*

> *Your servant, Fra Martelli*

In thinking about Martelli's letter, I realized it was a manner of confession. Martelli was confessing that rather than just overhearing the plotting, he was involved in the discussions. I take him at his word that he pleaded with the Grand Master for leniency and that he was overruled by Wignacourt's unbridled and vindictive rage and Fabrizio's overvaulting ambition.

Even though I really did not know Fra Martelli, by reputation he was thought to be an honest man. For that reason, I like to think that he came up with the escape plan as a way of getting Caravaggio out of Malta alive with the hope that he could find asylum somewhere. I must admit that sometimes I think it was to get Caravaggio off Maltese soil to protect the Order.

THE MAN WHO KILLED CARAVAGGIO

Martelli was passionately loyal to the Order, and he was a cagey politician. He also knew that his life was much endangered by what he knew.

The full truth about Fra Martelli and why he sent me the letter shortly before he died, I will never know. Reading about Dell'Antella confirmed what I knew. Without doubt, Wignacourt was a vindictive, double-dealing, cunning man. Sadly, I thought back on Caravaggio's short and unhappy life. Wignacourt was only one of many involved in the dangerous game Caravaggio's prodigious talent had placed him in all his life.

Ottavio Leoni, *Portrait of Caravaggio*, c. 1621

Author's Note

This book is a novel. It might even be considered an historical novel. However, it is not fiction.

For some years I have been researching the art of Caravaggio. That research provided me with many pleasures as I visited great museums in beautiful cities. My earlier work on Michelangelo brought me the opportunity to know Rome and Renaissance art in some detail. Pursuing Caravaggio, a bad choice of words given his fate, provided opportunities to visit and learn about Sicily, Naples, and Malta, and even a brief visit to the small village of Caravaggio near Milan.

Over the years, my interest in the psychoanalytic understanding of art, artists, and art history has provided me many contacts with artists and art historical, psychoanalytic, and museum scholars. On becoming acquainted with Caravaggio's art, it is not surprising that as a psychoanalyst interested in art and artistic personality, I became interested in the trajectory of Caravaggio's tragic life. In short, as I became more involved in the study of his art, I also became more involved in the study of him as a man.

A visit to Malta and Saint Paul's cathedral at Mdina

produced a treasure. Through fortuitous circumstance, I met a priest who was interested in my work. He took me deeply into the bowels of that immense cathedral into a large room where were stored numerous leather-bound ledgers—records from the Inquisition in Malta. Although the Inquisition was abolished when Napoleon came to Malta and its records were ordered destroyed, some clever Maltese hid them away in the Mdina Cathedral where they are preserved.

There they were—over-sized, beautifully bound leather volumes. The priest selected one, and on opening it showed me the meticulously hand-written original, verbatim transcription of the interrogation of Caravaggio by the Inquisition shortly after he arrived in Malta, an event that appears in a minor way in this book. I suspect that in Rome and Naples there are other long-forgotten verbatim accounts of the many arrests and trials of Caravaggio, his fellow artists, and their street friends stacked away in voluminous legal archives waiting to be exhumed. What a treasury of revelation of their lives and language lies awaiting discovery.

In the Malta volume, Caravaggio was being interrogated about a minor matter, a case of alleged bigamy. I am sure you can imagine how exciting it was to read the account. By this serendipitous meeting, I was face to face with Caravaggio's words.

AUTHOR'S NOTE

It proved the rare opportunity to study Caravaggio's linguistic style. Through my able translator, I was able to get a feel for the man through his language. I might add that some of the language made the priest blush. Caravaggio and his artistic contemporaries were earthy people.

The interrogation of Caravaggio by the Inquisitor in my book is a highly fanciful version of what the priest translated for me; however, it is true to Caravaggio's style of thinking and language. I tried to capture Caravaggio's delight in tormenting the Inquisitor and artful dodging of questions that are clearly evident in the original transcript. Obviously, his many brushes with the law and the courts made him an expert in seeming to comply while giving little or no information. Of all my researches, in some ways, that brief encounter with Caravaggio gave me the clearest and I hope most accurate picture of the man.

Another revealing experience in my travels for this book was visiting the town of Caravaggio with an Italian colleague. Caravaggio, not too far from Milan, is difficult to find, even though it is clearly marked on the map. The little village is eclipsed by a nearby massive shrine, the Santuario di Caravaggio. It is striking that there is this gigantic memorial on the site where an apparition of the Virgin appeared to a young peasant girl, Giannetta de'

Vacchi, and produced a miraculous spring; yet, there is not a single indication that this is where one of the world's greatest painters spent his childhood.

Once we found the small village, through pure chance we stopped at its tiny museum to ask directions. The Museo Navale Dott. Ing. Ottorino Zibetti is devoted to the maritime collection of a former citizen. Again, there is no mention of the artist. To our astonishment, we learned that the elderly man in charge of the museum, Ottorino Pellegri, was married to the last surviving kin of Caravaggio. His wife's family is from Como, and she is descended from Caravaggio's sister Caterina. Caterina, who married a Signore Venizzoni, was the only sibling of Caravaggio who married and had a family. Sadly, the man and his wife have no children. They are truly the end of the Merisi line.

Signore Pellegri told us that there is nothing in the small complex of buildings that is directly related to Caravaggio nor is there anything or anyone in the area related to the family except his wife. He assured us that nothing remains of the family farm and that the family graves are lost in history. He did show us the church where he claimed that Caravaggio's parents were married. There, he pointed to a small painting that lore says fascinated the artist as a boy.

AUTHOR'S NOTE

His knowledge of his wife's famous ancestor is limited to the standard account, but he knew it well. He delighted in telling us a story about his wife. When she was age 4, her family went to Milan and visited a museum. They suddenly realized that the little girl was not with them. Alarmed, they searched the museum and found her sitting on the floor staring at the only Caravaggio painting in the museum. (Caravaggio is a town that honors the miraculous.)

I asked him about Maddalena Vacchi, Fermo Merisi's first wife. He responded that, "Maddalena died in childbirth." I wondered if there were a possible relation to Giannetta de' Vacchi, the girl to whom the virgin appeared. He shrugged and said, "She might have been distantly related to the peasant girl."

I was not surprised that Signore Pellegri minimized Caravaggio's homosexuality, mental disturbance, or any suggestion that he had been murdered, as he quickly added that Caravaggio's mother (his wife's ancestor) came from the Aratori family, "an old and well-established Caravaggio family." It was clear that the family still fears being tainted by some of the puzzling facts about the painter's life.

The visit gave a vitality and immediacy to the facts I had been gleaning about this strange man. Just as when one visits sacred places, I had that uncanny feeling of closeness to the events and a peculiar sense of reality regarding the persons involved. I kept thinking *I* am walking where Caravaggio walked as a boy, and *I* am sitting in a pew in which he very well might have sat.

This book evolved over years as I viewed Caravaggio's paintings and randomly gathered facts about them and his life. Gradually, I developed some ideas about his short and unhappy life and became fascinated with the mystery of his death. Because of the shortage and inconsistencies in the facts, it was with some reluctance that I decided to novelize them.

After some thought, I realized that Mario Minniti was the perfect voice for the events. Caravaggio and he came to Rome about the same time and met by chance. It seems clear that they met in the Piazza Navona where they both were hustling and where Caravaggio was painting small pictures to sell. We know they lived together for some time before Caravaggio was discovered by Del Monte and that Mario eventually moved in with Caravaggio in the Palazzo Madama. We know that Mario was Caravaggio's first model and that Mario learned to paint from him. It is also clear that Mario was replaced by Cecco as model and lover. We know that Mario was in Malta at the time Caravaggio arrived there, and according to the priest in Mdina, most now agree that Caravaggio's interrogation by

AUTHOR'S NOTE

the Inquisition in Malta was about Mario mistakenly labeled Greek. Of most importance, Caravaggio came to live with Mario when he escaped from Malta, and Mario played a critical role in the events in Malta immediately prior to Caravaggio's death.

I invented Mario to tell the story. However, he is not wholly invention in that I develop him from the small amount that has been written about him as a youth and later as a successful Sicilian painter. In that Mario died when he was 63, thirty years following the death of Caravaggio, I have him mature during the years, and I envision him as a man facing the end of his life burdened by his extraordinary experience with the great painter and wanting to leave for posterity a written record of that experience.

Mario and Caravaggio, like most of the non-noble characters in this book, were men of the street. They were educated by nuns, but they spoke in street-wise dialect. For his writing, though, I thought it best to use the language that the nuns taught Mario rather than his vernacular. It is he who is writing this account, and we all write differently from the way we speak. Also, it made the book a lot less smutty. However, where I invent quotes and discussions, I thought that it gave an authenticity if I used vulgarisms and decided to do them in Italian. I decided not to translate the vulgarisms and leave that to my reader's imagination.

THE MAN WHO KILLED CARAVAGGIO

For expert help in Italian vulgarisms, I turned to a young friend, an Italian artist, Milos Maiorana-Zahrodka, who has a very full and earthy vocabulary in English and Italian. At first we tried to find vulgarisms of the period and not those that have found their way into modern Italian. That turned out to be more difficult than we anticipated. The words we decided upon are largely present-day vulgarisms common to the Trastevere area of Rome.

Regarding sources, the Caravaggio literature is vast. However, primary sources citing the events of his life and death are sparse, confused, contradictory, and I suggest have been purposely obfuscated. His two frequently cited contemporary biographers are Giovanni Baglione and Giovanni Pietro Bellori. Both of the biographies follow the style of Giorgio Vasari's (1568) classic *Le Vite de' Più Eccellenti Pittori, Scultori, et Architettori*.

Baglione's (1642) *Le Vite de' Pittori, Scultori, Architetti* devotes only three pages to Caravaggio. During Caravaggio's lifetime, Baglione's writings and recorded comments show him to be an envious rival of Caravaggio. He is the last person who would present an unprejudiced view of Caravaggio, and that prejudice is easily apparent in the pages of his *Le Vite*. Even though his biography is filled with errors (in fairness, we must admit that Vasari was not always interested in accuracy and was not above personal biases), snide comments, and frequent condemnations with faint praise, Baglione's *Le Vite* offers important information regarding the chronology and vicissitudes of much of Caravaggio's life.

When it comes to Baglione's evaluation of facts regarding Caravaggio's death, one must be particularly cautious. It must be remembered that even though the book was published in 1642, the Caravaggio section was probably written in 1625, only three years after Wignacourt's death. In addition to Baglione's antipathy for and eagerness to defame Caravaggio, at the time of its writing it still would have been dangerous to question facts regarding Caravaggio's death.

Bellori's (1672) *Le Vite de' Pittori, Scultori ed Architetti Moderni* was published thirty years after the Baglione book. I think Bellori is more factual in presenting Caravaggio's many difficulties than other contemporaries. His biography is more extensive in details and praise than Baglione's. Convincingly, Bellori tends to see the adverse circumstances that constantly befell Caravaggio as due to the fact that his paintings argued successfully against the prevailing Mannerist style. Even more, his work provocatively defied the artistic prohibitions of the Counter Reformation. Bellori accurately notes that not only artistically but indirectly religiously

Caravaggio was a revolutionary. More openly than others at the time, Caravaggio's artistic realism defied the Church's attempt to control what people were allowed to see. Accurately, Bellori also adds that Caravaggio's problems were constantly aggravated by his "tormented nature."

All of the contemporary accounts of the final days are ambiguous and inconsistent and filled, I suggest, with purposely altered and omitted facts. Bellori's account of Caravaggio's final days unconvincingly, I feel, closely follows Baglione's. He accepts "unknown attackers in Naples," "mistaken identity resulting in an arrest in Port'Ercole," and death from "fever on the beach."

Subsequent accounts of Caravaggio's life and death are heavily laced with error and lore. However, in that Baglione's text is the most quoted account of Caravaggio's last days, in the book I use it as though it were the official record of Caravaggio's death.

The modern Caravaggio art historical literature is extensive, but it is mostly devoted to the study of individual art pieces, comparisons with contemporaries, and his influence on art in general. Unfortunately, a great deal of this is yet to be translated into languages beyond Italian.

Several modern publications were uncommonly helpful in augmenting my general knowledge of Caravaggio, his art, and his life. Through his study of primary documents, Maurizio Calvesi, the Italian art historian and essayist, more than any other art historian, continues to expand our biographical knowledge about Caravaggio. If Baglione were out to besmirch Caravaggio's reputation, Calvesi is out to salvage the "slandered painter." In *Caravaggio Bacon,* the catalogue for the remarkable exhibition in the Galleria Borghese (2010), Calvesi's chapter, "Caravaggio: The Excellent Art of a Slandered Painter," rather than seeing Caravaggio's work as iconoclastic, Calvesi rightly sees the paintings as artistic rebellion against prevailing Mannerism. However with scant evidence, he boldly rejects many biographic assertions about Caravaggio.

Calvesi's brilliant and moving descriptions of the paintings, really interpretations, unfortunately are heavily tinged with his belief that Caravaggio was dedicated to Oratorian belief. No where is this more clear than in his interpretation of the final *David with the Head of Goliath* seeing it as a cry for redemption rather than an agonal outburst of anger toward injustice, as I have Mario say.

Although Calvesi joins Baglione in asserting that Caravaggio "died of malaria infected while traveling through areas where the disease was rampant," he makes a slight nod to the mystery of the death by noting that Caravaggio "for reasons which are not clear, ended up in Port'Ercole." I also take encouragement from the fact that Calvesi agrees with me that it was probably Fabrizio Colonna who helped the artist escape from Malta, "a feat otherwise impossible from that unyielding island prison."

Peter Robb's (1998) *The Man Who Became Caravaggio* encouraged me in this undertaking. His is, as I hope mine is, a readable account. Too often, though, he presents conjecture as historical fact and inconsistencies are dismissed. In my novelized version, I try to indicate when I am interpreting and inventing facts by making my impressions into Mario's reminiscences. However, some of Robb's ideas are close to ones that I independently developed. These correspondences in conjecture gave me a surer sense of certainty (certainty is not to be confused with factuality) as I pursued the lapses, inconsistencies, and ambiguities, especially in developing a theory about Caravaggio's last days and death.

Helen Langdon's (1998) *Caravaggio, A Life* proved invaluable. Her volume is a scholarly, fair, and clearly written biography filled with interesting details and knowledge of Caravaggio's life, knowledge about which she admits is limited. Her work especially conveys much useful information about Caravaggio's contemporaries and his time.

AUTHOR'S NOTE

A consistently reliable resource was Howard Hibbard's (1982) encyclopedic *Caravaggio*. His careful and thorough research of the painter and the paintings is the gold standard. The Hibbard volume contains invaluable primary materials in Italian with English translation, including a full presentation in Italian and in English of the chapters about Caravaggio from Baglione, Bellori, and other contemporary writers. Unfortunately, his precision and reluctance to romanticize the artist or the art obscures much of the colorfulness of Caravaggio's life and times. In that he was an old friend and an esteemed colleague who disliked taking liberties with art and artists, I know he would object mightily to this novelized story of Caravaggio.

The Characters I Have Created

As I have developed them, the characters in this book are gleaned from fragments and information found in numerous sources. The personalities that I give them come from integrating those fragments of information with years of practice as a psychiatrist and a psychoanalyst.

Cavaliere di Giustizia

Poor Cavaliere di Giustizia's role in Caravaggio's murder is completely my fabrication, but someone had to lead the pursuit through Sicily and Naples, and someone had to entice Caravaggio on his ultimate journey. The only fact I have regarding Giustizia is that in some records it is stated that he was the knight whom Caravaggio attacked in Malta that led to the arrest and brutal confinement, although most of the accounts read ambiguously "a noble knight was attacked." The knights, Johannes Honoret and Blasius Suarez, are not my invention. The records of the time reflect these two knights as having been assigned "in a solemn ceremony" the task of recapturing Caravaggio.

<u>Marchesa da Caravaggio, known as the Marchesa Colonna</u>

Costanza Colonna in my book and historically plays a central role in Caravaggio's life. There is, as Mario comments, an uncanny parallel between Costanza Colonna and Vittoria Colonna, who was of great importance in Michelangelo Buonarroti's life. Unlike Vittoria about whom we know a great deal because of her importance to Renaissance poetry, what we know about Costanza is sparse. If she seems ethereal in the book, it is because historically we know little of her other than that she was long a guiding and protective presence in Caravaggio's career. As I attempted to develop her place in the story, I was struck by the fact that even such simple facts as who was her father, whom she married, and whether Fabrizio was her son or her nephew were unclear. In any

AUTHOR'S NOTE

case, the Marchesa Colonna remains one of many great women, like Vittoria Colonna, who in silent and innumerable ways fostered and made great art possible.

<u>Cecco (Francisco Boneri)</u>

Although Francisco Boneri, called Cecco, is an historical figure, little is known about him. I draw his personality largely from my imagination and somewhat modeled from information we have about Leonardo da Vinci's relationship with his sometimes model and "wild" young, beautiful, homosexual lover, Gian Giacomo Caprotti, called Salai.

Leonardo's fascination with Salai, which is Milanese slang for "little Satan," is well-documented. Leonardo referred to him as his greedy, lying, little thief, and for over twenty-five years suffered repeated verbal and physical abuses from his young lover. Yet Leonardo continued the relationship with Salai until his death, and Salai was listed as partial heir to Leonardo's estate. It has been said that Salai was an artist, but there is little evidence to substantiate this claim.

Cecco did become a painter of some repute in Rome following Caravaggio's death. In the manuscript, I have Mario describe some of Cecco's successes and the curious self-portrait in which he shows what he looked like, or what he thought he looked like, when he was in his early twenties. Striking in his self-portrait are hooded eyelids that do not appear in any portraits of him by Caravaggio. It would seem that not only did Cecco magnify his relationship with Caravaggio, calling himself Cecco da Caravaggio, but he thought he looked like him. Poignantly, Cecco painted from memory reappears in Caravaggio's very late painting, the horrendous 1610 painting *David with the Head of Goliath*.

Lena (Maddalena Antognetti)

The brief descriptions that I give of the important prostitute models of Caravaggio are largely based on facts known about the paintings and from legal transcriptions made at the time of the girls' frequent appearances in the courts of Rome. It was from the transcriptions of their frequent appearances in various courts that provided the full picture of their lusty language and hot-tempered manners.

I am probably giving Lena, the lovely Maddalena Antognetti, a larger place in Caravaggio's affection than she deserves, but it does seem that their relationship was unusual. Lena bore the name of Caravaggio's father's first wife, Maddalena, who died in childbirth. It is not difficult to imagine that as a specter of tragic woman, the dead wife played an important role in Caravaggio's psychology. Further, there is a sweetness and tenderness in the way

AUTHOR'S NOTE

Caravaggio painted Lena, a sweetness also found in his paintings of beautiful Annuccia and Fillide. The importance of Caravaggio's carrying Lena—*Mary Magdalene in Ecstasy*—with him until the very end of his life is something I impute.

Some accounts say Caravaggio was Lena's pimp, for which there is no evidence. Actually, there is no evidence that Caravaggio pimped any prostitute, male or female. Some report that he fathered a child with Lena, the child in *La Madonna dei Pellegrini,* who later is the Jesus in *La Madonna dei Palafrenieri.* In fact, Caravaggio met Lena after the child's birth, the child being 3 or 4 years old when he appears in *La Madonna dei Pellegrini.*

Fra Antonio Martelli

The good brother, we know little about. I give him a central place in the story that he does not deserve. However, he is one of the few highly placed Knights of Malta whom we know had intimate contact with Caravaggio and Wignacourt. Also, Martelli seems to have been an honorable man. However, making him a part of the decision about what to do with Caravaggio and making him the one who recognizing the viciousness and vengeance of the Grand Master pleads for leniency for the great painter is of course pure invention on my part. In order to understand his silence once the dastardly task was decided and began to be implemented, I also had to invent that he, as a loyal knight, was bound by his vow of obedience. To make him a fuller person, I do have him indicate that much of his silence was out of fear for his life, and I do have Mario recognize that it was also self-serving.

Martelli's letter to Mario, of course, is pure invention, as was the idea that it was written out of heart's comfort. Yet other than out of guilt, it is difficult to understand why he agreed to protect Caravaggio in Messina, unless he was just another of the many who exploited this great talent.

Fabrizio Colonna

If I had to apologize to anyone, it would be to Fabrizio Colonna. Truly, Fabrizio is unfairly maligned. He was closely related to the Marchesa. Some indicate that he was her son; some say that he was her nephew. Yet, it is fact that the Marchesa Colonna did communicate with Wignacourt requesting he consider asylum for Caravaggio. It is also fact that Fabrizio was a general in the Maltese navy and close to Wignacourt when Caravaggio was in Malta. It seems most likely that Fabrizio organized the escape from the *guva* and was able to provide a waiting ship for the escape to Sicily. However, it seems implausible that he risked his status with the Grand Master to help Caravaggio out of friendship or loyalty, so I had to give him a nefarious motive.

AUTHOR'S NOTE

I draw Fabrizio's character largely from clinical psychiatric experience. We are too familiar with lawless youths who make personality conversions and become solid citizens. In their conversion, these now solid citizens often have a righteousness. Yet paradoxically, they easily rationalize conscienceless acts. Often these young men are engaging, and they effectively and subtly manipulate others with charismatic clarity. With unsurprising frequency, they insinuate themselves into positions of high rank and authority. Often, they skillfully ride the coattails of an important older man who is enchanted with their cageyness and personableness.

Grand Master Alof de Wignacourt

I do not apologize for my portrayal of Grand Master Wignacourt. He is constructed largely from facts. He did become enormously wealthy by organizing raids on the Arab merchant fleets, by taking and selling slaves, and by endearing himself to European nobility through giving safe haven to their errant progeny. Records often note his particular "fondness" for pages. That he would see and use Caravaggio as a vehicle for self-aggrandizement is not difficult to imagine.

All evidence points to the fact that in Malta Caravaggio got into serious trouble with a very highly placed person who had the power to control, distort, and destroy important records. It is also clearly documented that Wignacourt went to extraordinary lengths to obtain a papal pardon for Caravaggio.

Without question, at that time there was political interest in demonstrating power and prestige through acquiring great art, and Caravaggio was one of the most, if not the most, acclaimed artists in Italy and in much of Europe. I do not think it is too far-fetched to assume that Wignacourt saw an opportunity to add to his majesty by granting Caravaggio asylum and wanted to keep him in Malta for the prestige carried by having him there and amassing his art. It therefore seems highly likely that Wignacourt's putting himself on the line with Pope Paul V for Caravaggio would have been accompanied by an agreement that Caravaggio remain in Malta. There also seems ample evidence that Caravaggio worked behind Wignacourt's back to secure a pardon through Cardinal Borghese and wanted to return to Rome.

Regarding Caravaggio's trial, most of the reports at the time express the sense of excessiveness in the Order's response to what seemed like a frequent and rather insignificant event, a fight between two knights. Atypically for the Order, the court record no longer exists and probably was destroyed at the time. If the record were destroyed, this suggests that Caravaggio's infraction, whatever it was, was responded to vindictively and was covered up, most likely by someone very highly placed. I think it is fair to assume that Wignacourt was outraged to learn that Caravaggio was working behind his back and insincere in agreeing to stay in Malta. I believe he vindictively responded.

Regarding the role of the page in these matters, I fully admit that it is my invention. Although it is weak evidence, I do see the page as being more interested in Caravaggio than in Wignacourt in the portrait of the Grand Master. If Caravaggio did not seduce the page and cuckold Wignacourt, it certainly seems that Caravaggio wished he had.

Cardinal Francesco Maria Borbone del Monte

Del Monte looms large in this book, a place he well deserves. Although Italian, he was remotely descended from the royal Bourbon dynasty of France and always maintained a pro-French bias. He served the De Medici and Sforza families in highly important diplomatic positions and was at one time considered a candidate for elevation to pope. There is some evidence that his association with young boys as well as his French sympathies defeated that candidacy.

Besides his role in Caravaggio's life, he was a profound man interested in science, music, literature, and especially the arts. He was an active patron of all three and gave many intellectual salons that introduced and helped many artists. He actively and openly helped Galileo.

I drew upon many sources from my clinical work to create his character, especially his homosexuality. I imagine him to be a man who struggled with homosexuality all his life, finally coming to a partial acknowledgement only later in life.

I think of Del Monte as having a specific but not rare kind of homosexuality. As he grew older, his "fondness" for boys and young men was strongly motivated by a narcissistic desire to re-live his life vicariously in their young bodies. This often played out in pathetic ways.

I see him particularly involved in and delighted by the sociopathic antics of the boys he gathered around him. He marveled at what they did and what they got away with—things that unconsciously he wished he could have done.

His homosexuality, to my mind, had a strong masochistic bent that allowed him to take much abuse from Caravaggio and repeatedly compelled him to come to Caravaggio's rescue regardless of personal risk. I see his relationship with Caravaggio and probably numerous other boys and young men as a kind of love that was a mixture of masochism, altruism, and loving protection.

AUTHOR'S NOTE

<u>Mario Minniti</u>

Mario, as I designed him, may be a fairly accurate representation of who and what he was. There is ample evidence that as a boy in Sicily he was considered "wild." There is no evidence that he showed artistic talent early or that he had any training in art.

He was a hustler in the Piazza Navona when he came to Rome and in Rome he met Caravaggio. He moved into the Palazzo Madama with Caravaggio and was Caravaggio's model and lover until Cecco came along. I extended the friendship as continuing after Caravaggio and Cecco moved into the Palazzo Mattei. Without evidence, I have Mario continue occasionally as a model and an assistant to Caravaggio, and without any evidence I make him the master of the now famous copy of *The Betrayal of Christ* and of the mysterious fate of the original.

All agree that Mario was in Malta when Caravaggio arrived there. Some records suggest that the Inquisition regarding the alleged bigamy in Malta concerned a "Greek artist." Others thought the record confused Greek with Sicilian. As already mentioned, my priest interpreter said that most now agree that the man in question was Mario.

Without doubt, I gave Mario more closeness to information

than is warranted and may have made him a more honorable and truer friend than he was. I probably had him mature more than he did. However, we do know that he married and became an acknowledged artist. Because Mario was there at the beginning, some of the middle, and close to the end of Caravaggio's life, I think he is the person most likely to know the fullest if not the most accurate story.

In that Mario is a painter and my narrator, I use him to give my responses to some of Caravaggio's greatest works. It is not my purpose to describe or allude to all the works. I have the excuse that Mario did not see them all. (Also, I agree with Mario that there are many copies, duplicates, and misattributions.) The book is not about Caravaggio's paintings but about what the paintings and the circumstances of the paintings add to understanding the drama and tragedy of this man and his life.

Michelangelo Merisi, known as Caravaggio

Clearly my Caravaggio is largely imagination anchored in contemporary accounts, early biographies, verbatim court records, lore, and my fascination with his paintings. I attempt to balance the drama of Caravaggio's short and unhappy life, the colorful times in which he worked and lived, the majesty of the work, and the development of him as a person. I could not resist presenting a theory about his death, a theory that takes into account more of the facts surrounding his later years than his official biographers did.

My depiction of him developed from my psychoanalytic dealings with a number of young men, never as monumentally talented, whom I see as similar to Caravaggio. Assiduously trying not to do a "case study" and trying as much as possible to avoid the psychoanalytic lexicon, I came to see Caravaggio as a young man who suffered significantly from the early and unexpected loss of his father and grandfather when he was 6. I place importance on the fact that he was reared by a mother under trying times and suffered a second tragic loss with her death during his turbulent adolescence. As a psychodynamic response to these monumental losses, I suggest he developed a conscious and unconscious ubiquitous and unquenchable hunger for and a cataclysmic fear of relationship. Following his tumultuous youth and as he entered a parentless young adulthood, his quarrelsome, hot-tempered behavior defensively fended off his intense desire for and intense fear of close relationship.

Fueled by disappointments and fair and unfair punishments, frequently self-activated, his inner rage increased. At times, his rage explosively externalized, such as in the often-cited historical incident regarding the servant boy and the artichokes. Mostly his rage was self-directed resulting in moroseness, bitterness, provocativeness, and ubiquitous self-destructive behavior particularly when situations moved favorably for him. Success rather than bringing self-cohesion and a sense of mastery, affiliation, and certainty brought chaotic excitements that marginally defended against self-fragmentation and vulnerability. He was an exaggerated, really a psychotic, version of Sigmund Freud's "a character ruined by success."

Throughout his life, his wariness of relationships easily moved into suspiciousness. Magnified by the almost unimaginable circumstances of his last years, his suspiciousness reached malignant proportions.

Caravaggio's fear of closeness was fueled and perverted by his unsizable talent. Like many hugely talented people, he learned early that he could not truly know who wanted him as opposed to those who wanted something from him. His fragile self-image allowed laudation of his talent to feed a sense of privilege and exaggerated esteem and disappointments to produce abysmal despair and deep bitterness. As he was recognized and widely desired by the rich and powerful, his talent became his ever-present savior and simultaneously exposed him to vicious exploitation. In every sense, his talent was a blessing but also a curse that undermined any developing sense of trust.

With time and colossal disappointments, his inner rage increased and his art changed. With increasing exposure to the vindictive envy of many, his early artistic production of brightly colored, whimsical portrayals of the vagrancies of ordinary people became dramatic visualizations of some of the most wretched passages of the Old and New Testaments.

As his inner darkness increased, darkness dominated his art. Bright and illuminating external light became an inner ominous glow. As the master of *chiaroscuro* he became the master of painting darkness. I agree with Mario. Caravaggio's darkness is the darkness of night. In the darkness lies potential menace.

I completely invented the story of Caravaggio, Mario, and Saint Agnes. I did this because of the prominence of the Sant'Agnese in Agone in the Piazza Navona, Caravaggio's early Roman home, and my personal delight in the Sant'Agnese e Santa Costanza. Beyond that, I wanted to bring into broad profile the fragility of women and the brutality of men that dominate the art of Caravaggio.

As powerful and brutal as are the men in the *istoria*, Caravaggio's heroines are delicate, tender, and beautiful. Even when called upon to do horrible acts, as Judith is when she must behead Holophernes, Caravaggio's women exhibit the horror of what they are required to do. Rarely does one see such horror in Caravaggio's men as they brutalize other men. In the various *Flagellations* and *Crucifixions,* there is delight in torturing and serenity in being tortured.

I see Caravaggio and his exaggerated masculinity, provocativeness, quarrelsomeness, and violence as a defense against the frail, often brutalized woman who resided within him. How this might be related to identification with Maddalena, his father's first wife who died in childbirth, or a recapitulation of the relationship between Fermo and Lucia, his father and mother, is a psychoanalytic question that begs to and yet never can be answered.

In his inner struggling with conflicted concepts of male and female, I see the origins of Caravaggio's sado-masochistic homosexuality, a homosexuality that informed his art and gives it its unusual vitality. His painting gives us some of the most sensuous, androgynous boys and young men, some of the most serenely beautiful women, and some of the most dynamic, powerful, brutal, and tormented men that can be found in art.

In the end, I ask myself would I have liked the Caravaggio that I have created. I do not think so. I have known many like him.

AUTHOR'S NOTE

Although they are initially engaging, one quickly grows weary of their moroseness and self-defeating and subtle, and sometimes not so subtle, sadistic and masochistic manipulations, as I fear Del Monte did.

The story about Fra Francesco dell'Antella and its uncanny parallels to Caravaggio's experience seems made up, but it is historical. I, of course, made up the dialogue between Dell'Antella and Caravaggio about the *Sleeping Cupid* and Dell'Antella's seeking out Fra Martelli. However, that Fra Vincenzo Carafa, the Knight's Prior of Capua, had obtained and attempted to hold the paintings from the fatal boat and that their ownership was contested by Marchesa Colonna is historical and strangely rarely emphasized in the Caravaggio literature. I see Carafa's mysterious possession of the paintings "found" on the boat following the death of Caravaggio as adding great weight to the hypothesis that the Order was behind the murder plot.

An Ironic Link Between Napoleon and Caravaggio

One painting, *The Entombment*, has a curious history. In some ways its fate epitomizes the ironies associated with the vicissitudes of many of Caravaggio's paintings. When the *Palafrenieri* lost their chapel in Saint Peter's Basilica and sold their *La Madonna dei*

THE MAN WHO KILLED CARAVAGGIO

Palafrenieri to Cardinal Borghese, it seemed that Caravaggio's hope of ever having a painting in the Vatican had vanished.

However as part of Napoleon's plunder of Rome in the early 1800s, Caravaggio's *The Entombment* was taken to France. In 1815 with the downfall of Napoleon and the Congress of Vienna, as part of retribution, *The Entombment* was returned to Rome and given to the Vatican where it is now a major masterpiece in the Vatican's Pinacoteca. Ironically, it took the plunder of Rome by Napoleon to fulfill a dream of Caravaggio's.

Conclusion

The book presents the way I have put together meager, inconsistent, and greatly altered facts about a great painter and his art. Although Michelangelo Merisi existed, in lore there are many Caravaggios. In my novel, I invent a new Caravaggio, a Caravaggio derived from years of looking at his art, following his footsteps, and talking with art historians and artists comingled with years of psychiatric and psychoanalytic experience with art and with creative and less creatively endowed individuals.

An important purpose of the novel is to present a theory regarding Caravaggio's mysterious death. In attempting to solve the mystery, I have followed the inconsistencies in the reports and read into them what is there and tried to look for what is not there. Allowing for distortions of time and situation, I see Caravaggio's death as the eventuality of a vindictive old man who felt betrayed and humiliated by an monumentally creative young man.

The story of Caravaggio is tragic, but in it a greater tragedy is revealed. If the situation were as I have envisioned, the blind rage and vindictiveness of one powerful man, Alof de Wignacourt, deprived the world of continuing and maturing treasures from a great artist! If this is so, we are reminded how fragile creativity is and how often its fate is determined by an unscrupulous few.

Illustrations and Permissions

Cover: Caravaggio, *Portrait of a Knight of Malta* (Detail), 1607, Palazzo Pitti, Florence, Italy/The Bridgeman Art Library.

Chapter One: Caravaggio, *The Young Bacchus*, 1597, Galleria degli Uffizi, Florence, Italy/Alinari/The Bridgeman Art Library.

Chapter Two: Caravaggio, *Saint Francis in Ecstasy*, 1595, Wadsworth Athenaeum, Hartford, Conn./Art Resource.

Chapter Three: Caravaggio, *Victorious Cupid*, 1602, Staatliche Museen, Berlin/Alinari/The Bridgeman Art Library.

Chapter Four: Caravaggio, *Madonna di Loreto*, 1604-5, Chiesa di Sant'Agostino, Rome/Alinari/ The Bridgeman Art Library.

Chapter Five: Caravaggio, *Deposition*, 1602-4, Vatican Museums and Galleries, Vatican City, Italy/The Bridgeman Art Library.

Chapter Six: Caravaggio, *Flagellation*, 1607, Museo e Gallerie Nazionali di Capodimonte, Naples, Italy/The Bridgeman Art Library.

Chapter Seven: Caravaggio, *Decapitation of Saint John the Baptist* (Detail), 1608, Co-Cathedral of Saint John, Valletta, Malta/The Bridgeman Art Library.

Chapter Eight: Caravaggio, *David with the Head of Goliath*, 1610, Galleria Borghese, Rome/The Bridgeman Art Library.

Chapter Nine: Caravaggio, *Portrait of Alof de Wignacourt, Grand Master of the Order of Malta, with His Page*, c. 1608, Louvre/Peter Willi/The Bridgeman Art Library; Ottavio Leoni, *Portrait of Caravaggio*, c. 1621, Biblioteca Marucelliana, Florence, Italy/Scala/Art Resource.